Kiss of Death

An Al Pennyback Mystery

Charles Ray

ISBN:0615835554
ISBN-13:9780615835556

DEDICATION

To my granddaughters, Samantha Aeryn and Catherine Logan.
You are my inspiration.

Titles by Charles Ray

Al Pennyback mysteries

Color Me Dead

Memorial to the Dead

Deadline

Dead, White, and Blue

A Good Day to Die

The Day the Music Died

Die, Sinner

Deadly Intentions

Death by Design

Till Death Do Us Part

Deadly Dose

Dead Man's Cove

Dead Men Don't Answer

Death From Unnatural Causes

Deadly Paradise

Kiss of Death

Buffalo Soldier history series
Buffalo Soldier: Trial by Fire
Buffalo Soldier: Homecoming
Buffalo Soldier: Incident at Cactus Junction
Buffalo Soldier: Peacekeepers
Buffalo Soldier: Renegade

Other fiction
Angel on His Shoulder
She's No Angel
Child of the Flame
Pip's Revenge
Wallace in Underland
Further Adventures of Wallace in Underland: Wallace Saves the King
Dade Letter and Other Tales (a collection of short stories)
The White Dragons: A novel of international intrigue

Nonfiction
Things I Learned from My Grandmother About Leadership and Life
Taking Charge: Effective Leadership for the Twenty-first Century
Grab the Brass Ring
African Places: A Photographic Journey Through Zimbabwe and southern Africa

1.

"You can just call me Mouse," he said.

An unfortunate cognomen given his appearance.

The first thing I noticed about him as he walked into my office was that he was preternaturally thin. He wore a neon yellow shirt with a green vest over it and mauve pants that made him look like someone on the way to a 70s era disco party, and they hung on his gaunt frame like cloth on a wire rack. His skin and hair were almost the same color; a dusty brown like the hair on a hamster. His face was thin; close-set, brown eyes that darted from side to side, sunken cheeks, lips that were reddish brown and not too thick, and a thin nose, under which was wispy mustache that looked like two dark brown stains to either side of his nose; or like the whiskers of his namesake.

When Heather, my associate, had shown him into the office, she'd introduced him as Elwood Tucker, but he insisted on the nickname.

I extended my hand, which engulfed his thin brown hand. He was sweating. He shouldn't have been sweating; the air conditioning in my office was working, and I had it set on high to fight off the oppressive July heat outside.

I motioned to the plain wooden chair sitting in front of my desk and resumed my place in the larger, leather executive chair behind the desk.

"Okay, Mr. Tucker," I said. "What can I do for you?" Sorry, but I don't like using nicknames, and I especially don't like names that remind me of rodents. In fact, I hate rats.

He sat there, looking at me with his tiny eyes bobbing and his nose twitching like a hamster in a cage waiting for a treat. He kept bouncing his legs up and down, and tapping on his knees with his bony fingers – tap, tap, tapity-tap. "Uh, okay . . . yeah; see, it's like this. I got this problem . . . I need your help with."

Now, I sort of figured he was in my office because he had a problem. I don't get too many social visitors.

"I kind of figured you had a problem," I said. "Thing is, I don't get paid to figure out what your problem is; I get paid to try and solve it."

He cocked his bullet shaped head and looked at me with a question in his eyes. Sarcasm was lost on him. A hamster was smarter.

"Yeah, right . . . I guess you want to know what my problem is, right?"

I nodded. This was looking like it would be a long session.

He fiddled with the ends of his mustache, avoiding eye contact with me. It bothers me when people won't look me in the eye. I was beginning to wonder why Heather had passed him along to me; usually, she's pretty good at spotting time wasters, or the type of client I won't take. I trust her judgment – mostly – so, it bothered me that this one was beginning to look like one she'd let slip through the cracks.

At last, he looked up at me; squinting with eyes that were mere dots beneath his protruding brows. "It's like this, see," he said. "I work for this dude, Mr. O'Grady. He got a office over by the bus station." More fiddling with the mustache. "I sorta run errands for him see."

I held up my hand. He leaned back in the chair, holding his hands up in front of his face as if he thought I was planning to hit him.

"Look, I deal with legal issues. If you're looking for a change in employment, I'm afraid I can't help you. We're a two-person shop. Besides, I don't' need anyone to run errands."

"Naw, it ain't nothin' like that . . . well, it might turn out I be needin' to find another job; but, that ain't why I come to you. I got me a bigger problem than findin' a new job, man."

"Really; a problem that you need a private investigator for?"

"Well, it ain't exactly that either. What I be needin' is protection. I need me a bodyguard. I heard 'round the neighborhood, you be helpin' people what need protection."

"I don't know where you heard that. I do investigations only." That wasn't precisely true. I had done a bodyguard stint once – a young singer who'd been getting threats; her manager hired me to protect her while I also tried to find out who was threatening to kill her. It's not the kind of work I like doing, though. That case had not only nearly got me killed, it almost caused a breakup in my relationship with my girlfriend Sandra Winter.

"The folk what told me said you help people who need help, and man, I sho nuff in need of

4

help right now."

He had a plaintive, almost crying, tone in his voice, and his lips quivered. He looked pathetic. But, I figured him for a drug addict. For starters, his yellow shirt had long sleeves, and in July in Washington, DC, only dope addicts who shoot the shit into their arms and bureaucrats who wear jackets to work wear long sleeves. He was clearly no bureaucrat.

On the other hand, he had the pathetic, hang dog look of someone who was in trouble, and I'm a sucker for people in trouble, unless it's trouble they got into from doing something illegal. I was running all the possibilities through my mind as I looked across the desk at him. If he was jerking me around, I'd show him the door. But, the fact was, I wasn't working on anything at the moment, and he'd aroused my curiosity. I'm a sucker for puzzles. I decided to let him talk a little more so I could find out what was really on his mind.

"Okay," I said. "Tell me why a guy your age . . . you're what – twenty-eight or so – why would you need a bodyguard?"

"I be twenty-six, and I need a bodyguard 'cause somebody gone try to kill me."

"Why don't you just go to the police, then?"

He looked down at the floor, suddenly finding something in the vicinity of his shoes that was more interesting than me. I felt that tingling sensation at the nape of my neck that I get when someone's tossing male bovine manure in my direction – my bullshit meter was 'pinging.'

"Are you involved in something illegal? Because, if you are, you've come to the wrong place. I don't know what you think you know about private investigators, but aiding and abetting criminal activity is not one of the things they do; not if they want to keep their licenses."

"Uh, naw, ain't nothin' like that," he said without looking up at me. "I ain't done nothin' illegal, I swear. But, somebody tryin' to kill me."

I noticed that he appeared to be skirting answering my question. I hadn't asked if he'd actually *done* anything illegal. Of course, I thought, he could just be stupid and not understand me. "But, are you *involved* with anyone who's done something illegal?"

Now he looked up at me; well, at my chin; he still wouldn't meet my eyes. "Uh, well, it's . . . I mean . . . well, yeah . . . maybe."

"Is it yes, or maybe?"

"Okay, yeah, my boss, he sometime do things the law don't like. But, I ain't got nothin' to do with none of that, you dig. I'm strictly legit."

"So, you're legit, but you work for a guy who breaks the law? What is it you do legitimately for this guy who breaks the law?"

"Uh, see . . . he, uh loans money to people," he said. His eyes flickered up and he briefly met my gaze, but then just as quickly, dropped his gaze back to an area in front of his feet. "I just have to collect from folks what owe him. That's all I do, I collect the money they owe."

"You're a collector for a loan shark? And, you say you don't do anything illegal? What do you do about people who can't or won't pay?"

His Adam's apple began bobbing up and down. "Most folks on my route pay regular like. Payments ain't that high – all they gotta pay is the weekly vig see. If they can't pay, I talk to the boss, and sometime we can make arrangements."

The vig, or interest payments, on loans from loan sharks could come to more than the principal amount of the loan. Most loan sharks took a dim view of people who borrowed and couldn't repay; and, tended to respond rather aggressively as an example to others.

"And, when you can't make arrangements?"

"Uh, well, the boss, he got other dudes who deal with that."

"So, when you can't collect, your boss sends someone else around to break fingers or bust kneecaps?"

He jumped as if someone had shot an electric current through him. It didn't take a PhD in psychology to know that had hit home.

"Yeah, but like I said, most of my customers make the payments on time. I only had one problem lately. This chick's kid got sick and she needed money to pay the doctor bills. Then, she got laid off from the store she worked in up in Wheaton and couldn't make her payment this week . . . that was yesterday; I always collect on Monday, 'cause people usually done had a good weekend and they don't got no excuses 'bout needin' money for partyin' and such."

He tapped a little beat on his bony knees, still studying his shoes.

Then, he continued, "She's a nice lady, and her kid, a girl, is cute as a bug. So, I felt sorry for her, see. Anyway, I didn't want to report her to Mr. O'Grady, so, I jacked the vig up a few points on a few of the other customers; not so much they'd have reason to complain, you know; and, I used that to cover her for the week. But, some sumbitch musta complained to Mr. O'Grady, 'cause when I delivered my receipts to him last night, he put ordered a hit on me."

"Whoa, friend," I said, holding up my hand.

"You mean to tell me, your boss ordered you killed, and you walked out alive? Did he actually say to someone he wanted you dead? Why didn't you go to the police?"

"I done told you, I don't like dealin' with the cops and, naw, he didn't point to some dude and say, kill Mouse, but he ordered a hit all the same."

I shook my head. "I'm afraid you've lost me, Mr. Tucker. If he didn't say he wanted you dead, how do you know he put a contract out on you?"

"I know 'cause when I give him my receipts, he ask me a whole lot of questions 'bout how much from who, and shit like that. Then, he reached up and pulled my head down and kissed me right here." He pointed to his left cheek. "That his way of markin' you for a hit. He done kissed me right in front of all them dudes what hang 'round his place. Fucker done give me the kiss of death."

2.

I restrained myself from laughing at him long enough to see that he was as serious as a train wreck. When he said he'd been given the 'kiss of death,' he'd meant it literally.

According to Tucker, O'Grady, who had been brought to the U.S. from Ireland when he was six, and had decided to become a career criminal in his teens, was obsessed with the Marlon Brando character in *The Godfather*. He aped Brando's speech, mannerisms, and dress, and ran his tiny criminal operation as if it was a Mafia kingdom, with him as *Don*, or overboss, underbosses, lieutenants, and soldiers. Tucker, as a collector on loans, was a soldier, one step up from the numbers runners, and just below the loan collectors who were also enforcers. O'Grady was also, Tucker said with trembling lips, given to the dramatic gestures of the Mafia, such as leaving a dead animal on someone's doorstep to express displeasure, and, the thing that had sent Tucker scurrying to my door – the *Kiss of Death* to mark those in the organization who were to be eliminated.

It was all very interesting, but still, not enough to get me involved, until Tucker got into the nature of O'Grady's activities. In addition to numbers, loan sharking, and drugs, he ran prostitution in the area near the Washington Naval Station.

"I been workin' for Mr. O' Grady since I was seventeen," he said. "And, I ain't never had no problem with workin' for him 'till I met Lila Logan."

When he spoke her name, he got a goofy expression on his face, a lopsided smile and his eyes went unfocused.

"Lila; I call her Kitty; is the most beautiful woman I done ever met. And, we hit it off right away, even though I was there to collect on the money she owed Mr. O'Grady. She just a sweet person, you know. Anyway, we started seein' each other regular like, and I could tell she liked me as much as I liked her."

Now, his expression became sad.

"Then, she got laid off at the place where she work, and she was havin' trouble gettin' the money to make the weekly payments on the loan. Now, Mr. O'Grady, he got a strict rule 'bout that. You make the vig payment every week, or he send one of the enforcers to talk to you. The baddest is this dude name Billy Clark. He a cracker from somewhere down south and the dude got ice water for blood. I think he like hurtin' people, you know. So, anyway, to keep Lila from havin' to deal with him, I started padding the vig for some of the other folk on my route, and usin' the extra to pay hers."

"Weren't you worried that one of the people you were boosting might tell O'Grady?"

"Tell you the truth, I didn't think 'bout that. I just wanted to keep Lila safe. But, I guess that musta happened, 'cause Mr. O'Grady told me one day that he'd heard rumors 'bout it, and it had to stop. I tried to argue with him 'bout it, but he just told me to shut up and do my job, or he'd turn her account over to Clark. Then, I heard he'd called Lila in and told her he could make a deal with her 'bout her payments."

"Who did you hear that from?"

"Lila told me. I'se thinkin' maybe he done asked her to turn tricks for him. He keep a stable of women at his office building over by the Navy Yard, and runs the ladies what work out of the hotel next door. Now, Lila done had a hard life; she been on the street since she got pregnant when she was fourteen and her old man throwed her out of the house. I didn't like it, but I figured if that got her loan paid, we could live with it."

I frowned at him, and he must have noted it, because he cringed.

"Look, man, she's full growed, and got a right to do what she want. It ain't like she ain't been on the street before. But, that wasn't what that fat fuck wanted. He wanted her to give him her daughter."

Now, it was my turn to cringe inwardly. "What do you mean, give him her daughter?"

"Jennie; that's Lila's daughter; she had her when she was fourteen. She done good by her, too, seein' that she go to school and all, and makin' sure she got good clothes and enough to eat. Lila don't want Jennie to have to work the streets like she did, but O'Grady want her to ennertain his *special* clients. I never knowed for sure what was goin' on upstairs at the place. I mean, I know some of the girls have rooms up there where the Johns can go after gettin' a buzz on in the bar; but, he got some special rooms up there where he keep young girls for dudes who swing that way."

"This guy's prostituting underage girls?"

"Yeah, man. Now, I ain't got nothin' 'gainst a little paid shag now 'n then, but what kinda dude want to do a little girl? Hell, Jennie ain't even got tits yet. I mean, it just wrong, you know. Anyway, I started skimmin' from the other accounts to cover Lila's vig. Somehow, word musta got back to him. Now, he want me dead."

Elwood Tucker didn't impress me. A petty thug, he'd probably spent most of his life on the streets, and had a flexible sense of ethics; I had little doubt that he'd probably done violence at some point, and the fact that he could so casually discuss his girlfriend becoming a hooker, placed him near the bottom of humanity's ladder in my book. But, he at least did have lines he didn't seem willing to cross. Like a lot of career criminals, he didn't believe in hurting kids, so that kept him from being at the very bottom of the ladder.

I'd been on the verge of turning down his case; one less piece of trash for the cops to clean up, I figured. But, when he told me what O'Grady intended, it caused my blood to boil. Pedophiles that prey on kids are bad enough, but the scum bags that facilitate it, and get paid for it, are even worse.

I would take Tucker's case; not because I particularly cared whether he lived or died, but because I wanted to bring O'Grady down – and, bring him down hard.

3.

Since opening my private detective agency a decade earlier, along with being on retainer to the law firm of Holcombe, Stein and Chang, chasing down deadbeat clients and locating missing heirs, I'd taken a few cases on the side; usually cases involving people for whom the system was unresponsive.

My name is Albert Einstein Pennyback, thanks to a mother who had a thing for the German scientist, and wanted her only son to grow up to be famous like him. By the time I started high school, though, everyone called me Al. Not because they were kind or considerate, but because I'd had a growth spurt that first year of high school and was good with my fists.

I disappointed my mother by joining the army right out of high school. My father, a

World War II veteran, was more sympathetic, but only supported me silently – he was a tiger in combat, but always caved to her.

I went on to get a commission in the army after a few years, many of them in combat situations; married a beautiful girl from the Philippines who blessed me with a beautiful son. Then, Sarah and Ethan were taken away from me when Ethan was only six when a truck driver ignored a stop sign and plowed into the van Sarah was driving, killing them instantly. I was assigned to the Pentagon at the time, working my way up the army career ladder, but, devastated after losing my family, I quit the army. After moping around feeling sorry for myself for weeks, I let my old army buddy Quincy Chang talk me into getting my private investigator's license and opened a little one-man agency. He helped me out by convincing his partners at Holcombe, Stein, and Chang to put me on a ten-thousand-dollar a month retainer to do odd investigative chores for them; and I supplemented my income by taking the odd case that came in over the transom.

Over-the-transom cases were often facilitated by my assistant, Heather Bunche. I'd hired Heather right out of secretarial school, because she needed a job, and I needed someone to do the paperwork which I hated. She turned out to be a genius at coaxing information out of a computer, and had a network of former secretarial school classmates and friends all over the Washington, DC area, giving me access to information that was often unavailable to regular law enforcement agencies, so I'd quickly moved her up from secretary to associate. I couldn't give her extra salary, but whenever we got a windfall fee, I shared it with her in the form of a bonus. The rest of our income was plowed back into the business – I lived on my army retirement pay, which was adequate, given my relatively Spartan life style.

Before Tucker left the office, I had Heather type up a contract. He didn't even blink when I told him my services cost two hundred a day plus expenses, and that I'd need a deposit. He paid me a thousand in cash, crumpled bills he'd carried in his pants pocket. I didn't ask him where the money had come from. I advised him not to go back to his place. He told me he had a cousin in Damascus, Maryland, who lived on a small farm just outside the town. None of his associates in O'Grady's gang knew about the cousin, he assured me, so he should be safe there. I gave him my card and told him to call me or Heather when he got to Damascus and give us a contact number so I could keep him updated on the case, and he left.

Heather and I were sitting in the outer office going over the case.

"So, boss," she said. "What's your next step?"

"For starters, I'd like to know more about Tucker personally; and, as much as we can dig up on O'Grady."

She smiled brightly. I'd been preparing her to get her PI license so she could be a full partner with me, but she wasn't all that excited about street work. Computer research and working the phones were what she did best, and she was never happier than when she could take nothing more than a person's name and after a few hours of research, prepare a full bio on him. And, one of Heather's full bios would have made the CIA jealous. The woman could find things in nooks and crannies of the Internet, or in someone's Rolodex file that even the authors had often forgotten.

I left her happily pecking away at her keyboard and peering at the screen, and went back into my office.

By the time I was ready to leave the office around four thirty in the afternoon, she'd presented me with two neatly typed sheets; one for Elwood Tucker and one for Seamus O'Grady. I folded them and stuffed them into my pants pocket to read at home.

4.

Sandra and I were still decompressing from a harrowing trip to Hawaii to attend Quincy's cousin's wedding at a resort on the island of Maui – an event that had been disrupted by a sniper, hired by the groom's brother, who tried to get to the 'death do us part' of the ceremony early.

Sandra Winter is a teacher at Carter High School in Southeast DC, a tough, inner city high school whose students come from some of the roughest neighborhoods in the city. She and I met when I was investigating the shooting death of one of her students at the request of the murdered boy's grandmother, and after a rocky start had hit it off. Even though she still owned a small house in Takoma Park, she hardly ever stayed there anymore, more or less moving in with me at my renovated farm house just off River Road near Potomac, in Maryland's Montgomery County.

Our relationship was comfortable; we shared genuine mutual affection, and tacitly accepted that it was exclusive, but, neither of us was ready to take it beyond that. I still had issues surrounding the loss of my first wife, Sarah, and my six-year-old son Ethan, and Sandra had a thing about maintaining her independence.

School was out, so Sandra had had the whole day to herself. For me, though, school was never out. July 2, Monday; first day of the month, meant Heather and I would have to balance the previous month's books – well, it meant that Heather would have to do it, but, when she finished, I would have to look at them, nod as if I really understood what all those columns of figures meant, and sign off on it. All that while handling whatever work Quincy's firm might toss our way, and protecting Elwood Tucker from his boss. You'd think that would be enough, right? Oh, no. July 3, Tuesday, was my birthday; the birthday I'd been quietly dreading – I'd turn fifty.

Sandra had been working with Heather and my very short list of friends; Buster and Alma Mayweather, Quincy Chang, Lucy Mendez, Carlton Raine, and Elizabeth Sung completed the list; to put on some kind of party, despite my protestations.

When I walked into the living room, she was sprawled on the floor, writing on a huge sheet of butcher paper. I'd been prepared to be grumpy with her because of the birthday party, but the sight of her beautifully rounded rump encased in tight brown shorts, and the expanse of midsection exposed because her T-shirt had ridden up, drove any grumpy thoughts from my mind. She looked back over her shoulder at the sound of the door opening.

"Hey, birthday boy," she said. "How was it today?"

I told her about the Tucker case. When I got to the part about child prostitution, her face turned red. "You are going to go after this guy, aren't you?" she asked.

"Oh, yes I am. Protecting Tucker is just tangential. My main mission is to destroy O'Grady's operation."

The smile on her face when I said that was feral. Sandra's very anti-violence, but, like me, she viscerally hates those who exploit the weak, and a dirt bag who sexually exploits children is the lowest of the low in her book.

"I hope you make him suffer when you do it," she said simply.

I didn't have to respond. The look on my face told her all she needed to know. She simply nodded.

We prepared supper and ate it sitting on the couch in the living room listening to an NPR news program. After we'd finished eating and cleaned our plates, I sat at the table in the kitchen and spread the papers Heather had given me out before me.

The one on Elwood Tucker was scanty. But, he was only twenty-six, so there hadn't been all that much to find. It was much as I'd surmised from my visual inspection of him; he'd been in and out of trouble since his twelfth birthday, with arrests for vandalism and shop lifting mostly, spending most of his days on the streets instead of in school, finally dropping out in the eighth grade and going to work running errands for the older thugs who ruled the streets in his neighborhood. He'd been caught with two bags of crack that he'd been delivering for a local dealer when he was fourteen, and had spent a year in a juvenile detention center. After being released, he'd gone to work for O'Grady's organization as a debt collector for the crime boss's loan sharking operation. Three-quarter of a page was all it took to outline his aimless life thus far; a petty criminal, doing petty jobs for bigger criminals; a dead-end life with few signs of hope.

The information on Seamus O'Grady, on the other hand, filled two pages. O'Grady had emigrated from Ireland as a child, living first in New York, then Baltimore, and finally, ending up in Washington, DC's hard-bitten Southeast District when he was twelve. He'd attended the then mostly-black schools where, by the time he graduated, he'd made his mark with the black gangs who controlled the streets. By the time he was twenty-one, he was the second in command of one of the gangs, its only white member. Two years later, when the gang leader mysteriously disappeared – and, there was speculation that his body was somewhere in the murky bottom of the Anacostia River, O'Grady was the unrivaled leader.

A fan, even at a young age, of American gangster movies, he patterned his style of leadership on such notable gangsters as Al Capone and other Mafia head men. According to police reports that Heather had been able to access; and, I was careful never to ask her how; he'd been deeply impressed with the *Godfather* movies, the Marlon Brando character in particular.

Now in his mid-sixties, he'd run his gang, which unlike other gangs in the area had no name – it was just known as 'The Family' – for more than forty years. In the early years, some of the young, up and coming black thugs had challenged the 'whitey' for leadership. Every challenger met a grisly end; and, in several cases, even the members of their immediate families had been killed. Eventually, his method of handling competition, coupled with the largesse he bestowed upon those deemed loyal, caused him to be left alone. Even neighboring gangs, black, Latino, or Asian, tended to leave the area around the Naval Station alone. O'Grady's response to competition was to eliminate it – with extreme prejudice.

There had been speculation that, in addition to gambling, loan sharking, prostitution, and protection rackets, O'Grady was involved in human trafficking, including forcing underage girls into prostitution, but the authorities, local and federal, had never been able to obtain evidence linking him directly to any of the crimes he'd allegedly masterminded. The code of silence around him was like a hermetically sealed dome – and witnesses who were not part of his mob were bought off, intimidated into silence, or suffered fatal 'accidents' before they could testify.

Sandra had come into the kitchen while I was reading about O'Grady. She stood behind me, reading over my shoulder. I could feel the quivering of her body as she read, and occasionally, she would gasp quietly. When I finished reading, I turned and looked up at her. Her deep blue eyes glistened.

"My God," she said. "How is it an animal like that can operate for so long with impunity?"

I took a deep breath and folded the papers. I then pulled her around onto my lap, holding her close and stroking her back.

"I imagine this is just the tip of the iceberg, babe. I'll bet there's a ton of payoffs to officials that Heather hasn't dug up information on yet."

"If he's able to operate right under the noses of the authorities for this long without being punished; how do you think you have a chance to do anything about him, Al?"

How indeed? O'Grady would be a tough nut to crack, but, I intended to crack his nuts and crack them good.

"I have a few advantages the authorities don't have. First, I can't be bought. Secondly, unlike the honest officials who I have no doubt would bring him down if they could, I don't have to worry about his Miranda rights, his right to privacy; in fact, as far as I'm concerned, this piece of shit has *no* rights I'm bound to respect. He's like an animal in the jungle. And, like a jungle animal, he's now my prey."

I said it evenly, without a trace of emotion, which belied the way I was feeling deep inside. I was declaring war on Seamus O'Grady, and there would be no Geneva Convention to protect his ass.

"You know, Al," she said quietly. "When you talk like that, you almost scare me."

"Sorry, babe; I don't like to expose you to this. It's not you I want to be scared. I want him to be scared."

She nuzzled her head into the crook of my neck and hugged me hard.

"If he's not scared, he has to be the

stupidest man on the face of the earth."

I doubt that he'd be scared; not at first. I also didn't think he was stupid. Just over confident. He'd been king of the hill for a long time, and probably thought he was invulnerable. But, like any human, he'd have a weak spot. It would be up to me to find it, and when I did, I planned to bore in like a tsetse fly and then, make him regret that he'd ever been born.

5.

The next morning, I drove to the office early. I popped my head through the door to let Heather know I was running an errand and would probably be gone for several hours. She was still busy looking for more dirt on O'Grady, so she just looked up at me quickly and waved, and then turned her attention back to her computer.

I didn't tell her where I was going. No sense in worrying her.

I decided to leave my car in the lot in front of the office. My '85 Mustang GT, with the glossy white exterior and black upholstery, which I bought to replace the old brown Volkswagen bug that I'd driven for more than ten years, that had been blown up by some white militia in West Virginia a couple years earlier, would stand out in the Navy Yard area like a pimple on prom night. I walked up Fourth Street to the Waterfront Metro Station.

The Green Line train from Waterfront, heading east toward Branch Avenue in Prince Georges County, Maryland by way of Navy Yard, was crowded with morning traffic, a few sailors in their summer whites, naval officers in tans, one or two business men, tons of laborers, and far too many students on their way to school. The students weren't as loud and boisterous as they would be later on their way home from school, but, that still left them loud enough to drown out the tinny voice of the driver as she announced stations.

Fortunately, I only had to go one stop to Navy Yard station. I exited the station near First Street, walked a block north to L Street and turned right toward Second Street.

The block was a collection of hulking buildings, except for the one-story structures which seemed to squat defensively, in soot-streaked red brick, graffiti-smeared gray concrete, and one or two wooden structures that looked as if a stiff breeze would send them flying off in all directions. The sidewalk slabs canted and dipped and had large chunks gouged out here and there, making little craters filled with limp yellow weeds and stagnant brown water.

Across the street from where I stood was a two story red brick building. The first floor was windowless, and there was a recess in the center, in which I could see a heavy green wooden door. Six windows on the second floor were covered with black drapes. There was no sign anywhere on the building that gave a clue as to what it was for or who was inside. To the left was a four story hotel, *Isle of Bliss*, also a red brick building, separated by a six-foot wide alley. To the right was a weed-strewn parking lot in which several expensive looking cars were parked.

On my side were a newsstand, a liquor store, and a small combination drug store/convenience store. I stopped at the newsstand. An elderly man with mahogany skin and a round head covered with white peppercorn hair, his bowling ball-size paunch hanging over his belt, sat on a stool behind the counter. In addition to newspapers, magazines, and lottery tickets, he sold candy, cookies, snack crackers, and soft drinks from a cooler behind his stool. I picked up a copy of the *Washington Post* and tossed it on the counter.

"That be all?" he asked.

I bought a chocolate candy bar and a can of orange soda. The soda can was icy cold against my hand. I tore open the candy bar and took a bite. Folding the paper under my arm, I stepped to the side. Another elderly man, completely bald, his dark chocolate skull gleaming with sweat, sat on a wooden fruit crate against the wall of the liquor store. He had a large can of malt liquor in his gnarled right hand.

Looking up at me, he scooted over on the crate and nodded down. There was just enough room for me to sit, but our hips would have been touching.

"That's okay," I said. "I'll just stand here." I stood with my back against the wall.

"Suit yourself. Ain't like old age's catchin' or somethin.'" He took a deep pull from the can, and then wiped the flecks of foam from his lips. "You ain't from round here."

Not a question; a statement; but, not particularly hostile or challenging – just a statement of fact. He looked like the type who knew everything about the neighborhood. My luck was running good. With him sitting there, I had a good cover for watching O'Grady's place without drawing too much attention to myself. At the same time, I could probably learn a lot from him.

"Yeah, I just moved to DC from Texas," I said, which was true except for the *just* part. I know I have a slight twang in my voice, so he might actually buy the lie. "Been moving north ever since the construction industry in Houston went bust; finally come up here looking for work."

The old man chuckled and looked up at me. "Boy, you done come to the wrong place, 'less you gone work for the guvmint. They ain't got much work in the construction industry these days, and most of what they got go to them guys what come up here from Salvador and places."

"Looks like somebody is doing well," I said, pointing at the expensive cars parked among the weeds.

A look of distaste crossed his face. He cocked his head and looked up at me again. "You ain't gone be wantin' to mess wit them folk cross the street, son. Ain't nothin' but trouble they is."

"What kind of trouble?" I asked innocently.

"Aw, you name it, them boys git up to it. They strong arm most of the shopkeepers for protection money, run drugs and numbers, and that hotel," he pointed to the hotel across the street. "That belong to them. They rent rooms by the hour. The ladies of the evenin' entertain they customers there."

"In other words, they're a criminal gang."

"Ain't you been listenin', boy? That what I just said."

"I got a friend down in Texas who has a cousin here in DC. I heard he worked near here. Maybe you know him; his name's Tucker; Elroy

. . . no, Elwood?"

"Yeah, I know him. Scrawny, rat-faced boy; they calls him Mouse." He shook his head. "He growed up on these here streets. Been in 'n out of trouble since he was a young pup. Yeah, he work over there. I think he collect money for the loan sharkin' operation. Your friend know what he been up to?"

"No, I don't think so. He just said his cousin might be able to help me find a job, is all."

"Well, boy, you take my advice; you steer clear of Mouse and his friends. They ain't nothin' but trouble. You be better off goin' over to the Greyhound station and gettin' on the first bus headin' south."

I took a sip of the orange soda, which had quickly gone flat in the heat of the morning sun. The candy bar had started melting, so I stuffed it into my mouth and washed it down with a slug of the warm, sticky sweet soda.

"I might; but, before I go, I should at least say hello to my friend's cousin, just in case he called him and told him I was coming."

"Well, I don't advise you goin' over there to do it," he said. "You know, I ain't seen Mouse 'round here last few days. He got a ratty apartment t'other side of the Navy Yard. Maybe you find him there."

"Yeah, I'll do that." I pushed away from the

wall. At that point, a large, silver Lincoln Town Car pulled up in front of the building opposite us. A large, very dark man, wearing a gray suit that strained over his massive shoulders, got out of the front passenger seat and looked suspiciously up and down the sidewalk. After a few seconds, he leaned over near the back window and nodded.

The door opened and an even larger man, bald headed and florid faced, got out. He was draped in a bright blue suit, unbuttoned across a huge stomach. The black man stepped back, still scanning the street and sidewalk, as the fat white man waddled toward the recess in the center of the building. When he'd disappeared into the shadow of the recess, the car backed up and pulled into the parking lot, quickly disappearing around the corner of the building.

I looked down enquiringly at the old man, who was looking back at me with an expression of bemusement. "You wonderin' who that is, ain't you?" I nodded. "That there be Mr. O'Grady. He the boss of the gang what hang out over there. Run ever thing for near six block 'round here, and been doin' it for long's I can remember. They all bad over there, but he the baddest of the lot. You wants to stay clear of him."

"Isn't it a bit unusual for a white man to be running things like that in a black neighborhood?"

His laugh was husky. There wasn't a lot of mirth in it.

"Most parts of this town that'd be a true statement. Mr. O'Grady, though, he kind of a special white man. He Irish, but he been raised in the projects with the black kids, and he act more like a black man than he do a white – 'cept when he actin' like one o' them Eye-talian gangsters. Man all mixed up in his head; don't know what he is. I do, though. He plumb evil is what he is. You smart, you stay away from him."

"Thanks for the advice," I said. "I think that's just what I'll do." I thought no such thing, but I wasn't about to discuss it with a stranger, no matter how well meaning he might be.

I drained the last of the lukewarm soda from the can and began looking around for a garbage can.

"You don't mind, young fella," he said. "I'll take that can offen you. After I finish my malt liquor, I plans to chew me some tobacco, and that can just perfect for a spittoon."

Since there wasn't a trash can in sight, that save me having to try and talk the clerk into taking an empty can – not that I had a snowball's chance of hell in being successful at that. I handed him the can, and he pulled a wicked looking folding knife from his pocket and began cutting the top off. I crumpled the candy bar wrapper and stuffed it into my pocket, which earned me a smile and nod from the old man. Guess he didn't see too many people in this neighborhood who wouldn't just drop it on the sidewalk. I returned his smile and walked off, heading east toward the Navy Yard; in the direction I knew Elwood Tucker's place to be. If he noticed that I wasn't going back the way I'd come, he said nothing.

Tucker's apartment was in a three-story brownstone building, huddled between two gray concrete buildings that looked like they'd once been warehouses, but were now just abandoned derelicts with smashed windows that the owners hadn't even bothered to board over. It was about five blocks from O'Grady's headquarters. I moved to the opposite sidewalk when I was two blocks away, looking around idly as if I was lost and couldn't find an address. What I was really doing was looking out for signs that Tucker's place was being watched.

And, half a block away, I saw that it was. Two young, tough looking black men sat on the ledge of what had been a store front window in an abandoned building diagonally across from Tucker's place. They were talking, slapping hands, and trying to look as if they were just hanging out, but the way they kept swiveling their heads to watch the front entrance of the building – one of them was always eyeballing the place – they might as well have put signs around their necks announcing their activity.

They didn't pay me too much attention when I passed them; another sign that they were there for a purpose other than just hanging around. I circled the block and headed back to the metro station.

I hadn't learned much more than I already knew, or suspected. The surveillance of Tucker's place seemed to confirm what he'd told me – I could think of no other reason someone would be watching. I also noticed the bulges in their baggy pants as I passed them. They were packing; probably .38s or 9 millimeters; and I had no doubt what they would do if Tucker showed up.

I'd promised him I would try to protect him. I'd promised myself that I'd bring Seamus O'Grady down. Looked like there was a conjunction of the two missions; if I destroyed O'Grady, there would no longer be any danger to Tucker. It's neat when things fit together like that.

6.

By the time I got back to the office, I was regretting not having taken the Mustang. Even though it was just ten in the morning, my shirt was soaked through with sweat, and my skin felt gritty from the dust that stuck to the sweat on my skin.

Heather looked up as I entered, looked down, then back up, her face wrinkled in disgust. "Good grief, boss; what did you do, go to a sauna?"

I made a growling noise at her. Something unintelligible, that I wouldn't want my mother to hear. It didn't help that I felt sticky and stinky. I went into my office and stood under the air conditioning vent. The cold air felt good, and I could feel my shirt quickly drying.

After a few minutes, Heather poked her head

around the door and sniffed the air.

"You can stop that," I said. "I'm okay now."

"Why do you insist on walking outside in this city in the summer?"

"It's hard to do foot surveillance without walking."

"Foot surveillance of what?"

"O'Grady's territory or course; what else would I be conducting surveillance on?"

She winced. "You sure that was such a good idea? I haven't found much really new on this guy; just more rumors of people he doesn't like sort of disappearing."

I had to laugh. If there was anyone who knew that I never took risks without first assessing the situation, it was Heather. She'd been with me from the beginning. White supremacist militia groups, Chinese gangsters, and bungling burglars had all had their shots at me and failed. Maybe it was hubris, but I just couldn't see a fat slob like Seamus O'Grady posing that significant a threat.

"That's the reason for surveilling the target, Honeybunch," I said. "So you can find the weak points before the target has a shot at you."

"Did you find his weak spots?"

"Uh, well, not yet. But, I'm working on it."

Now, it was her turn to laugh. "Which means he's guarded tighter than Fort Knox, right?"

I shrugged. "That just rules out a frontal approach." I decided to change the subject. "I'm gonna call Buster and invite him to join me for lunch. Anything else about O'Grady's operation I need to know?"

"No, other than like I said; there are rumors that people who've crossed him have disappeared."

Well, that's that, I thought. I went into my office and called my DC police buddy, Buster Mayweather and asked if he could meet me at Mom's on Sixteenth Street. Of course, I knew he'd be able to. Buster always has time for Mom's one of the District's best and oldest soul food places, run by a heavyset, no-nonsense southern black woman who runs it like her private dining room with all the diners being her 'chilluns' who better behave and eat all their food or else.

As he usually does, Buster beat me there. He was already hunched over a plate of food at our regular table in the corner, where we could keep an eye on the inside of the diner and the sidewalk outside as well, and where I could sit with my back to the wall. Mom sat in her usual place behind the cash register just inside the entrance, dressed in a tent-sized blue dress with a red and white checked apron barely encircling her massive waist. Her reddish-brown hair had been permed and heat treated, and glistened under the fluorescent ceiling lights.

The smells of frying meat, boiling greens, and baking cornbread hung in the air. Artery-clogging thought it might be it made my mouth water.

Mom smiled her wide, gap-toothed grin as I approached.

"Hey, hon; ain't seen you in a while. Where you been keepin' yo self?"

"I was out of town." I didn't want to tell her that I'd been trying to limit my visits to her establishment. Sandra had reminded me on more than one occasion that, now that I was approaching middle age, I needed to watch my cholesterol.

"Well, you just get yo self on over there with yo friend, and I'll bring you some vittles."

I knew better than to ask Mom for a menu. She had them, of course, but only for strangers or people she didn't like very much. Everyone else took what she put on the table for them. In all the years I'd been eating in her place, though, I'd never had a bad meal – a few cases of heartburn from all the grease, but never a bad meal.

Buster barely looked up as I flopped down in the chair adjacent to where he sat. He didn't have his back to the wall, but was still sitting where he could eyeball the restaurant and the street, which, despite his apparent obsession with the food on his plate, I knew he was doing.

"Hmmph sel set fud day gud," he mumbled around the mouthful of fried chicken he was chewing.

"Didn't your mother tell you not to talk with food in your mouth?"

He frowned up at me, finished chewing and washed it down with a big swig of iced tea. "I said set down, the food today's good. And, don't you be talkin' 'bout my mama. You know she taught me manners, but I was hungry."

"Hey, don't go ghetto on me, pal. You know I wasn't insulting your mother. I just know she taught you not to talk with your mouth full."

"He be tellin' nothin' but the truth, Buster Mayweather," Mom said as she sat a plate heaped high with fried chicken, collard greens, sweet potatoes, and a hunk of golden corn bread down in front of me. "And, you know I don't like bad table manners in my place neither, so you better behave."

"Yes, ma'am." Buster said. "Can I get a slice of apple pie with ice cream?"

She put her hands on her ample hips and

stared down at him. "What you suppose to say when you wants somethin'?"

"Please," he said meekly.

"Now, that's better." She reached over and rubbed his bald brown head. "It's so much better when you act mannerly."

She smiled and waddled off in the direction of the kitchen.

Buster shook his head. "Man, if the food here wasn't so good, I don't think I'd be takin' all that grief," he said quietly so she couldn't hear. He then turned to face me, all signs of meekness gone from his craggy face. "Now, what you want, bro? Not that I got any objection to comin' here for some good soul food, but you only invite me when you want something."

"Guilty as charged," I said. "What can you tell me about a two-bit gangster named Seamus O'Grady?"

He was just about to shovel another forkful of sweet potatoes into his mouth. He stopped, the fork halfway to his face, and stared at me.

"Why in hell you want to know 'bout that dirt bag?"

I told him about Elwood Tucker's fear that O'Grady had put a contract on him, and had hired me to keep him alive.

"Jeez, Al; first you got to get yourself messed up with a dude what can't decide whether he Irish, black, or Eyetalian, but you got to make it worse by takin' on one of his thugs as a client. Man, you need to get a better class of people to help."

"I know Tucker's a crook, but he's minor compared to O'Grady. Besides, I can't just stand by and let someone get killed – not even slime like Tucker. So, what can you tell me about O'Grady?"

"I can tell you you don't want to be messin' with him. Every DA since I been a cop has tried to get something on that dude, but nothin' sticks. Witnesses either get forgetful, or go missing. He been into everything illegal over in the area 'round the Navy Yard for as long as I can remember. You wouldn't think a white dude could be a big boss in a neighborhood that's ninety percent black, but O'Grady's been in charge forever."

"I've heard that he deals in trafficking young girls into prostitution."

"Yeah, been rumors of that, but ain't never had no witness come forward." He put his fork down and rubbed his chin. It made a raspy sound. "Say, is that why you goin' after this dude? 'Cause he turnin' young girls out on the street?"

"Can you think of a better reason?"

"Naw, guess I can't. Look, I can't tell you a whole lot; just that this dude's dangerous, so you got to watch your back, you dig. When I get back to the precinct, I'll see if I can find out anything else might be useful."

"Thanks, Buster. Anything that might show me his weak points would be useful."

"I don't think he got no weak points, man."

"Everyone has a weak point; I just need to find it. And, when I do, I'm bringing him down."

"Shit; I don't think I need to be hearin' no more. I'm an officer of the law after all. I don't wanna hear what you plan to do to this dude."

I smiled. "Don't worry, pal. You know nothing. Now, eat your chicken so Mom can bring you that apple pie and ice cream."

7.

After we finished our meal – and, the apple pie looked and smelled so good I had a slice with a big mound of vanilla ice cream on top – I decided to touch base with Lila Logan, Tucker's girlfriend.

She lived on the third floor of a run down, four-story, red brick apartment building in Southwest DC, on Seventh Street near E Street, just north of the Southeast Freeway. Like many of the neighborhoods in the area, this one had seen better days – long past. Trash littered the cracked sidewalks, and rusted hulks of cars and pickup trucks were parked illegally along the potholed streets. There were four apartments on each floor, with a rickety stairwell in the center. The floors and stairs were also liberally covered with empty beer cans, crushed cigarette butts, and crumpled newspaper.

I gingerly made my way up the stairs to the third floor. Logan lived in apartment 3B, the second unit on the right. I could hear the scuffling sound of footsteps inside as I rapped on the flimsy door.

"Who is it?" a female voice said from behind the door.

I held my PI license up in front of the peephole. "My name is Al Pennyback," I said. "I've been hired by your friend, Elwood Tucker. May I come in and speak with you?"

I heard the clicking of deadbolts and the rattling of chains, and then the door opened about six inches. Lila Logan must have been all of five-three, her pixieish face, bisected by a rusty door chain, was turned up and she peered suspiciously at me through amber-colored eyes. Her skin was smooth and the color of caramel, and her hair was straightened to a fare-the-well and tinted with reddish streaks.

"You say Mouse hired you? What he hire you to do?"

"I'd really rather not discuss it standing here in the hallway, Ms. Logan."

"How I know you tellin' the truth? Maybe you just tryin' to get in here so you can rape me or somethin'."

I could hear the scratching of faces against wood and the scuffing of shoes on the wooden floors in the other three apartments. It hadn't been my intent to share my business with the whole building – bad enough that my visit would be the talk of the place for days. I leaned in close to the door, lowering my voice so that hopefully only Lila Logan would hear. "Look, Ms. Logan, your boyfriend's afraid his employer, Seamus O'Grady, is planning to do him harm because of the debt you owe. He hired me to protect him. He also thinks you and your daughter . . . Jeanne . . . might be in danger, so I'm just here to check to make sure you're okay."

There was a long pause. She swayed back and forth as she continued to peer up at me. Then, she shrugged and the chain rattled as she removed it and opened the door. "Okay, come on in. Where is Mouse, anyway? He ain't been 'round in a coupla days."

I squeezed past her into the tiny living room. She stood there holding onto the edge of the door for a while. She was short all right, with small conical breasts pushing against the Washington Redskin's sweater she wore. A little heavy in the hips, but not grotesquely so, with shapely legs from hip to ankle, encased in a pair of shiny blue pants that looked painted on. Except for a light pink tint on her full lips and a hint of purple eye shadow, her face had no makeup. I could see how Tucker would have become smitten with her – she had a sort of slutty-innocent girl next door out for action look about her. Then, I noticed her twin sitting on the sofa staring at me. Well, not exactly her twin, this version had no lipstick or eye shadow, smaller hips, and no breasts, and the pants didn't curve as much.

"You must be Jeanne," I said to the girl on the couch.

She nodded, and looked imploringly at Lila Logan, who had closed the door and was now standing beside me.

"Yeah, this my baby," she said. "Now, what you want?"

"Well, Ms. Logan; like I said; your boyfriend hired me to try and keep this O'Grady character from killing him or harming you or your daughter."

"Now, if that ain't just like Mouse to be so worried 'bout us. By the way, you can call me Kitty. That my stage name back when I danced in the clubs."

I looked at her, my eyebrows raised.

"Oh yeah," she continued. "I did a bit of, you know . . . exotic dancin' . . . for a while." She frowned at the wide-eyed girl on the sofa. "Don't you be givin' me that look, missy; it kept food on the table."

"I ain't giving you no look, mama," the girl protested.

"You just be sure you don't." She turned her attention back to me. "See, when Jeanne here was little, I did what I had to do, but now that she growin' up . . . well, . . . I have to do regular work. Problem is, I got laid off my job, and I needed money for rent and food, you know. So, I done borrowed from that old white man. I was meanin' to pay it all back, soon's I got work. But, times hard right now, and companies ain't hirin' like they used to. Anyway, when I got behind on my payments, Mouse, he helped me out. He done some bad things in his time, but he a good man deep down."

I wasn't in a mood to argue with her on that point. For all I knew, Elwood Tucker was a saint who had just taken a wrong turn somewhere. I'd promised to try and keep him safe, and I'd do it. Keeping her and her daughter safe was just part of the package.

"When O'Grady found out he was cutting you a deal, I guess he didn't like it. Tucker says O'Grady put a hit on him."

"That don't surprise me. That one mean white man – 'specially since he always tryin' to act colored, you know. I sho hope he don't kill Mouse. He the closest thing to a daddy Jeanne every known."

"He said O'Grady offered to make a deal

with you regarding your unpaid loan?"

Her face wrinkled in disgust. "Yeah, that fucker done offered a deal, all right! He want to turn my baby out. He do that over my dead body; and, I done told him so."

"From what I've heard about this guy, he wouldn't hesitate to do just that. And, if you've challenged him, you're in as much danger as Tucker. Is there somewhere you and your daughter could go that people around here wouldn't know about?"

She laid a finely manicured finger on her cheek, her eyes screwed in concentration. Then she snapped her fingers. "I got me a cousin up in Damascus, Maryland. Ain't nobody 'round here no 'bout her. I think she let us stay a while with her."

"Good. Don't waste time packing too much. Hopefully, I'll have this whole thing settled in a few days."

"How you gone do that? The po-lice done tried to put that man away for years and ain't done it."

"Let's just say I don't operate under the same rules that the police do, and leave it at that. Now, you get packing. When I leave, lock the door and don't open it until you're ready to leave."

On my way out, I gave her one of my cards

and told her to call me if she had any problems.

Her daughter hadn't moved from her position on the couch.

8.

I spent the rest of the day, unproductively, in the office. Heather hadn't been able to come up with any more useful information; we had no other pending cases; and, I was still working over in my mind how I would approach Seamus O'Grady.

Oh yeah, and I was in a funk over the fact that today was my birthday. I'd just turned fifty, and so far, no one had even mentioned it. I know I'd been telling everyone that birthdays weren't important, and Sandra had sensed that I wasn't all that happy at approaching the big five-O, but damn it, you only get one birthday a year, and since I never celebrated Christmas, and everyone knew it, they could have at least humored me.

I was in a right stinking mood when I drove

home around five. The traffic sucked more than usual. The sun was still high in the sky – in July it sets around nine in the evening – when I shoved open the door into the living room.

"Happy birthday, Al," Quincy Chang said as he walked in from the kitchen.

"Happy birthday, darling," Sandra said, as she walked up and pulled me close, planting a deep, wet kiss where it mattered.

There was more 'happy birthdays' and 'many happy returns' and shit like that, but I was just standing there in the middle of the floor with a big shit eating grin on my face. They hadn't forgotten after all. Shit; I felt like the dumbest asshole in the world. Like Sandra would forget such an important day. Then, I felt really dumb for not noticing any preparations and being caught completely flatfooted.

"Uh, ah, wow; thanks, guys." Sometimes I surprise myself with my verbal ability.

"Gotcha, bro," Buster said, punching me in the chest. His playful jabs can break a rib if your chest isn't heavily padded with muscle – fortunately, mine is. "Betcha you didn't see this comin', did you?"

I wanted to say something smart ass, but could only stand there with my mouth open. He was right, I *hadn't* seen it coming. Some detective I was. Sandra saved me by planting another sloppy kiss on my lips.

"Come on," she said. "Who cares about all that? I've been slaving away in the kitchen all day getting things ready. Let's party!"

And, party we did.

Sandra had pulled out all the stops; making my favorite dishes, like chili con carne with jalapeño peppers chopped up in it, corn bread with sweet corn, and a large pitcher of lemonade. In addition, for a change, Buster brought beer rather than just drinking mine – four cases of *Dos Equis*, one of my favorite Mexican beers.

Heather, who'd come just after I did; she hung back at the office so as not to give the surprise away, and then followed me when I left; gave me a big coffee mug with 'World's Best Boss' emblazoned it in Old English script. Buster and Alma, who'd found a baby sitter for the twins for a change, gave me the three-volume set on the Civil War by Bruce Catton. Carlton Raine and Elizabeth Sung decided to leave their lair and join civilization, and they jointly gave me a framed print of Asian horsemen playing some kind of game with a sheep's carcass. The way Heather cringed when she saw it made me decide it would replace one of the hunting prints in my office. Quincy handed me a check for ten thousand bucks, and apologized for not buying a present. Hell,

I'll take money any day, and he knows it. He just apologized for the benefit of the others.

I was standing at the edge of the sofa, spooning chili into my mouth, when Sandra walked over and linked her arm in mine.

"I have two presents for you," she said softly. "One you get to unwrap after everyone leaves. The other will take a few more days."

I swallowed the chili and kissed the end of her nose. "I think I know what I'll be unwrapping, but what's the other one?"

"You'll just have to wait. It's a surprise."

"You know how I hate surprises, babe," I said. "Can't you at least give me a hint?"

She cocked her head to one side, batting her long lashes at me. Her smile was a bit crooked – the pixie in her. "Okay, a hint . . . uh, let's see; how about this? It's something you'll love, something you always loved, like an old friend."

Well, that helped not one bit, but the determined set of her jaw said it was all I was getting, so I went back to eating my chili, washing it down with beer instead of lemonade. Someone, I think it was Elizabeth, suggested dancing, which drew boos from everyone else – with Carlton booing the loudest. So, we ate and drank some more.

It was after ten when the beer finally ran out

and there was nothing left in the chili pot but stains. I yawned and stretched my arms, which got a laugh from Buster.

"You ain't foolin' nobody, bro," he said. "I know you ain't sleepy. You just want us to get our tails out of your house."

It was crude, but it worked. After a few more 'happy birthdays' and kisses from the ladies, everyone straggled out – they went out through the kitchen to get to their cars, which had been parked in the back yard near the barn. Then, I remembered the tire tracks I'd seen when I came home. Real observant, Al, I thought. If it had been an invading army, they would have snatched me before I knew what was happening. I wasn't sure if it was that I was getting old, or was just distracted by everything that was happening.

After everyone was gone, Sandra took me by the hand and pulled me into the bedroom, where I unwrapped my first present. It quickly became apparent that age wasn't my problem.

Charles Ray

9.

Sandra and I played a little game we sometimes play; we call it bedroom baseball. I was just getting ready for the second inning, having made it to third base and prepared to slide head first to home plate – when, the damn phone rang.

"Shit," we said in unison.

I rolled over and snatched the phone from the bedside table. "This had better be important," I snarled.

"Uh, I'm sorry to be botherin' you so late, Mr. Pennyback," Elwood Tucker's squeaky voice came from the receiver. "But, I done got myself into a bit of a mess, and I need yo help."

The green numerals on the clock read,

12:45. If he wasn't in real trouble, he'd soon be, calling me at that hour. "What kind of trouble could you be in at this hour?"

"Well, see, I left some cash stashed in my crib, and I thought I might need it if I gone be layin' low for a while."

"Damn, why would you go back to your place? You had to know they'd be watching it."

"Hell, I ain't stupid. I know they watchin'. That's why I waited 'till midnight. I snuck in through the basement. I guess they musta heard a noise or somethin', 'cause they just now comin' up the stairs."

"Shit, man; there's not a lot I can do for you," I said. "It'll take me at least forty minutes to get there even breaking all the speed limits. Can you get out of the apartment before they get there?"

"Uh, I can hide in the crawlspace they use for the air conditioning. Plus, I done put me a heavy duty door on when I moved in, and it got three dead bolt locks. Take 'em more'n a hour to break through that."

"Okay, get yourself hidden. I'll get there as quickly as I can."

I didn't wait for him to answer. I just broke the connection and dropped the phone on the table. Sandra lay on her back, staring up at me with her soulful blue eyes.

"That a client in trouble?"

"Yeah, and big trouble this time. His boss has hit men after him, and the idiot went back to his apartment. Two of them are going after him as we speak."

As we spoke, I was rolling out of bed. I quickly pulled on my underwear and the dark blue jeans I'd been wearing. I took a black jersey from the closet and pulled that on, and completed my outfit with black cotton socks and my black rubber sole boots. Just in case, I strapped a K-Bar knife to my left ankle.

"Al, be careful. I know you hate guns, and you can take care of yourself, but you're going up against two killers with guns."

"Had worse odds, babe. Don't worry; I don't plan on taking any unnecessary chances."

I kissed her gently on the cheek.

"Keep it warm for me. I should be back in two or three hours."

The Mustang started on the first try, and the roads were almost empty except for a few late-cruising cabs and one or two graveyard shift workers, so I pulled up a half block from Tucker's place about forty minutes after hanging up the phone.

The sidewalk was empty and most of the lights in the building were out. Tucker's apartment was on the second floor and, like Lila Logan's building, there was no elevator. That meant taking the stairs. That meant going slow and easy to keep the creaking of the floor from signaling my approach. I locked the Mustang and loped up to the building.

As I figured, the front door was ajar. So much for building security. The entry foyer was dimly lit by a single bulb on the wall over the mall boxes. I could hear scuffling and banging on the floor above, along with gruff voices.

"Come on out, Mouse," a deep voice said. "You just makin' this harder than it gotta be."

"That rat fuck done put in one of them reinforced doors," another voice said. "It gone take all night to open this damn thing."

"Just shut the fuck up and let me work, Skeeter. Yo bitchin' in my ear ain't makin' this no easier. Why don't you go over there and watch the stairs."

"What for? Ain't nobody gone come outa they apartment."

"You go watch the fucking stairs 'cause I fucking tell you to watch 'em, nimrod. Now, get away from me 'fo I shoot you. I got to concentrate on openin' this fucking lock."

"Okay, Mo, but you don't gotta be so mean. You gone let me shoot the sucker when you open the door, right?"

I heard a grunt, probably of disgust, and some mumbled words I couldn't make out. Their chatter covered the minor creaking of the stairs. The loose boards made squeaking sounds despite my walking at the sides where they should have been soundly anchored. At the top of the stairs, I paused. I could hear the scuffle of shoes on the uncarpeted hallway as the one I assumed was Skeeter approached. I flattened myself against the wall, feeling it sag a bit under my weight.

A large shadow fell across the opening, followed by a body that was as large as the shadow. Massive shoulders above a massive paunch, all of this sitting atop tree-trunk legs that ended in ferry-boat sized feet. A large, melon-shaped head, as dark as polished mahogany and bald as the top of a mountain, with tiny, bloodshot eyes that didn't seem to focus on anything in particular as it swiveled from side to side. This, I thought, must be Skeeter; wonder where someone so large got a nickname relating to something so small? Everything about him was large – so large that the .45 automatic in his ham-sized right fist looked like a toy you'd get from a cereal box.

He was as dumb as he sounded, too. His attention was on the bottom of the stairs. He didn't even see me standing not a foot away to his left, pressed against the wall. His tiny brain probably didn't expect anyone in the stairwell, so his eyes didn't see me. He still hadn't seen me when I reached over and grabbed his right thumb with my right hand, while grabbing the barrel of the pistol with my left. At the same time, I brought my left foot up and kicked him in the shin, and followed that up with a knee to his groin. He was a big brute, and in a face-to-face slug fest, he would have eaten me alive. But, the shins and the groin are vulnerable regardless of size; and as I was doing damage to these regions, I pulled his thumb back until I heard a snap like a dry twig.

That got his attention. His little eyes squeezed shut and he opened his thick lips to squeal in agony. Before he could do that, I brought my right hand up and jabbed him in his Adam's apple. That cut off all but an 'urk' sound. I twisted the gun from his hand. The pains in his thumb, throat, groin and leg were getting to him. He began to sag toward the floor. I slammed the butt of the .45 against his temple to speed up the process. His body hit the stairwell with a dull thud and began a bumpy journey toward the bottom, head first. I knew there was a good chance he'd break his neck, but I still had an armed gunman to worry about, so I let him slide.

"What the fuck that noise, Skeeter?" the other gunman, Mo, called. "You done gone and tripped on the stairs?"

I pressed back against the wall, breathing slowly. After some more muttering, there was silence. I peeked slowly around the wall. A small, dark skinned man was on one knee in front of the apartment at the end of the hall. He was prying at the door with a large screwdriver. On the floor at his knee was a little cloth case with lock-pick tools. Apparently, Tucker's locks weren't located where the tools could reach them, so he was left with brute force. He was prying at the area near the hinges, trying to gouge away wood so he could reach the hinge pins. I could see a .38 police special in his belt on his right side.

As I moved slowly forward, keeping near the wall without touching it and allowing the whisper of cloth against it to give me away, I watched him. He held the screwdriver in his left hand as he worked at the door frame, so I decided I'd go for that side. That way, he'd have less room to move his left arm.

I was about four feet away from him when something spooked him, maybe some atavistic response from cave man days that warned our ancestors of impending danger, but, his head jerked around toward me. At first, he just stared; his mouth draped open; as if his brain couldn't process what his eyes were seeing. Then, he shook himself, dropped the screwdriver and grabbed for the .38.

It was too late. In the second or two that it took him to react, I'd covered that last four feet in two steps. As the gun came out of his belt and he started to raise it, I put my right hand over the butt, covering the hammer and part of his wrist, grasping tight and pushing down. With my left hand, I grabbed his right arm, pinning it to his side.

The sound of the .38 going off, at such close range, was like having your head in a bucket with someone banging on it with a metal rod. The explosion of the gunshot was followed quickly by a high pitched scream, and I felt his grip loosen on the pistol.

I glanced down quickly and saw why. The pressure of my grip had caused his trigger finger to tense and he'd triggered off a round. Unfortunately, he hadn't completely cleared his belt, and the barrel was pointing at the top of his foot. Fortunately for him, he wasn't using hollow points. The 400 grams of lead in the bullet drilled through his fancy running shoe, through his foot, and out through the sole of the shoe into the floor. A low velocity round, the .38 special made a small hole going in and coming out, but it had to hurt like hell. His white, blue and gold shoe had a dark, blood-rimmed hole in the top.

He'd lifted his foot, and was off balance. "Aw, Jesus, I done shot my foot off," he screamed as he hopped on his good foot.

I'd been forgotten. All he had on his mind was his mangled, painful foot. All of this took just seconds, but to him it must have seemed like an eternity. I kicked the gun away and slammed my left fist into his temple.

His screaming stopped. His eyes, which had been clenched shut in pain, flew open, and rolled back in his head. He fell back against the door and slid down into a sitting position. I grabbed his shoulders and moved him away from the door.

"Tucker, can you hear me?" I yelled

"Is that you, Mr. Pennyback? I heard a shot. What happened?"

"One of your friends shot himself in the foot. He's sleeping now."

"What about the other one? They was two of 'em."

"You mean the big one? He's sleeping at the foot of the stairs. Now, come on out so we can get out of here before he wakes up."

I was being optimistic. While he might have broken his neck when he fell, I wasn't depending on it, and he'd be in a foul mood when he woke up. The small one, now lying against the wall, wouldn't be in a good mood either, when he got his foot mended. The best thing for both me and Tucker was to put as much distance between us and this spot as possible.

I heard the snick of several locks and the rattle of a chain, and then the door opened. Elwood Tucker peeked around the corner of the door.

"Jesus, you done whupped the two of 'em. Man, you somethin' else. What kinda gun you use?"

"I don't use guns," I said. I showed him the .45. "I took this from the big guy just before I threw him down the stairs." I walked over and picked up the .38. "I plan to get rid of both of them. Now, let's get the hell out of here."

I tucked the .38 into my belt next to the .45. The weight of the two guns was uncomfortable. Tucker made an appreciative whistling sound as he followed me out into the night.

10.

At that time of morning, the streets were empty and quiet. It was too late for even the late-night revelers and too early for the garbage trucks. We made our way to my car. Once inside, I put the two pistols in the glove compartment. Just to play it safe, instead of going my normal way back home; pass the Mall and along Whitehurst Freeway to Canal Road, which would have been quicker; I drove northwest to New Hampshire Avenue and then north to I-495, checking my rearview mirror every few seconds to make sure we weren't being followed. On I-495, I took the outer loop west to the River Road exit and then home.

The sky was turning from purple-black to dark gray when we pulled up in front of the house.

"Man, you sho live out in the sticks," Tucker said. "You grow cotton or somethin' out here?"

I glared at him, a look he could see in the dim glow of the dash lights. "No, I don't grow cotton. I just like privacy."

"Don't reckon nobody wanta be comin' botherin' you way out here."

"That's the general idea."

I got out, and Tucker followed me into the living room. He looked around and made a whistling noise.

"Nice pad for a farmhouse," he said.

I ignored the compliment and the dig.

"You can sack out here on the couch for a few hours," I said. "Come sunup, I'm moving you to a safe house."

"Ain't this place safe? Hell, who'd think to look way out here?"

"I know a place that's even safer. Besides, you don't stay alive by taking unnecessary chances. If O'Grady finds out I'm working for you, it wouldn't take much for him to find out where I live."

He had no smartass answer to that. The memory of the previous hours was still fresh in his mind no doubt.

"This safer place; is it out in the country too?"

"Yeah, it is; a few miles past here in fact."

He shook his head. "I don't know, man. I ain't never really been outa the city before. I gots to have me some bright lights and city sounds, you know."

"Look, it'll just be for a few days. Besides, you hang around here, you'll get a dose of hot lead and a dark grave."

"You got a point. Okay, I guess I can deal. You got a pillow for this sofa?" Then, his mouth dropped open and his eyes went wide. "Uh, hello, beautiful; man, you didn't tell me you be shackin' with an angel."

I turned to see Sandra standing in the doorway, wearing nothing but a nearly transparent T-shirt and panties, her blonde hair all awry as she wiped sleep from her eyes.

"What the . . .," she said as her vision cleared and she saw Tucker ogling her. "Al; who the hell is this person?"

"Uh, babe, this is my client, Elwood Tucker.

I couldn't leave him at his place, so I'm letting him stay here until sunup; then I'm moving him out to Blood's place."

"Hey, what's this blood shit? Uh, sorry, lady, don't mind my language," Tucker said. He stopped admiring Sandra's body long enough to turn to me with a frown on his face. "That don't sound too good."

"Blood's the nickname of a friend of mine," I said. "You'll be safer at his place than gold bars at Fort Knox."

"Why he called Blood? He a black dude?"

"Yes, he just happens to be black," I said. I decided against telling him that Carlton Raine's race had nothing to do with his nickname. "He used to work for the CIA, so he's pretty good at defending himself and others."

"So, you'll be leaving at sunup?" There was ice in Sandra's voice. She looked at Tucker as she'd just found him stuck to the bottom of her foot and she couldn't shake him off. For his part, he'd resumed ogling her.

"Yeah," I said. "Why don't you go on back to sleep? I'll be in as soon as I get our guest settled."

She glanced down and two bright red spots blossomed on her cheeks as she realized how much of her luxurious flesh she was displaying. Whirling, she vanished back into the bedroom.

"Man," Tucker said. "You got yoself one fine lady there."

"Yeah, just pull your eyes back into your head and get some rest. When I say sunup, I *mean* sunup."

He chuckled, but there was a bit of a skeptical look in his eyes. I don't have extra pillows, so I just propped up one of the cushions for him, and found an old light blanket that I'd stored in the hall closet for some reason. He sniffed at the blanket, but pulled his shoes off, lay down and pulled it up around his chin anyway.

As I turned to go to the bedroom, he made a clearing noise in his throat. I turned back to see him peering at me over the edge of the blanket. "What do you want?" I asked.

"I just wanted to say thanks again," he said quietly. "You hadn't come, I'd be dead for sure."

"Just earning my fee."

I flipped off the light and went to the bedroom to try and mend fences with Sandra.

11.

Sandra wasn't too pleased at our unplanned house guest, but a little murmuring into her ear accompanied by a back massage got her to listen to my reasoning for bringing him. She knew I'd made a commitment to keep him safe, and at that time of morning I hadn't had a whole lot of options.

We finally dozed off huddled together with her head tucked under my chin and her firm breasts smashed against my chest. Hadn't been for our guest that might have led to something else, but after the way he'd ogled her body I didn't think the noise we would have made was a good idea – nor did she.

The sun rose almost immediately. At least, that's the way it felt. I'd no more closed my eyes and drifted off to sleep than I felt the warm rays of sun through the window poking at my eye lids.

"Hmph," Sandra said as I extricated my arm from beneath her.

She opened her eyes halfway and peered up at me.

"You don't have to get up," I said as I rubbed circulation back into my arm. "I've got to get rid of our guest. I'll be back in time to fix you a good breakfast."

"Hmph," she said and rolled over.

I slid out of bed and went quietly to the bathroom, where I showered and brushed my teeth, and spent a little extra time splashing cold water on my face to completely wake up. I decided to forgo shaving – I'd do that after breakfast. I pulled on the same clothes I'd worn the night before. They smelled a little gamey, but I figured Carlton would understand.

Tucker was as hard to wake up as Sandra.

"Lemme sleep just a little while longer," he

complained as I yanked the blanket off him.

"You can sleep later. Get up and get your shoes on. We've got to get moving."

"Damn, bro; you always this hard when you get up in the morning?"

I made a snarling sound. He jumped off the sofa as if he'd been stung.

"Okay, okay, I'm moving."

He put on his shoes and with his head hung followed me out to the porch. The sun was just about halfway up, casting long shadows from the trees around my house. The morning air was brisk. But, by mid-morning, the July heat would have set in. I took a deep breath.

Tucker hunched himself into the passenger seat next to me. I fired up the Mustang's engine and swung around, heading toward River Road, where I took a left and headed toward Blood Raine's place.

Except for an almost sub-vocal humming, Tucker was quiet as I drove. Out of the corner of my eye, though, I could see that he was taking in the passing scenery, which got more rural the further west I drove. His eyes went wide when I turned onto the dirt track that leads to Blood's place, a cabin surrounded by a hundred yards of cleared ground that borders on a thick forest of evergreen and hardwood, in which deer and other animals roam freely because no hunter would dare venture so close to Raine's fortress.

And, fortress it is. The cabin, made of huge cedar logs, is larger than it looks from the outside, and it is sturdy enough to withstand an assault from anything smaller than a Sherman tank. The doors are metal reinforced and his windows are thick, bullet proof glass with shatter resistant coating. He has an array of sensors surrounding the place and lining the road leading in, and monitors them at a console in a little room off his living room, so no one gets near without his knowing. In another small room he has an arsenal that's sufficient to hold off a pretty heavy armed attack, and he knows how to use every weapon in it.

Carlton 'Blood' Raine was one of the earlier black field agents hired by the agency, and he'd proved himself in the field, doing some of their dirtiest missions. His nickname came from the fact that his missions usually involved the shedding of copious quantities of blood – his targets. When he retired, he was one of the most respected of their agents, and still retained ties at Langley, ties that made it possible for him to get his hands on some of their new toys from time to time to field test. I never asked him how he did that, but from time to time, he'd let me use some new gadget if he thought it would help me on a case.

We'd become close – with me substituting for

the children he'd never had, as he'd never felt it
fair to burden a wife with his job, and had been
alone until I introduced him to Elizabeth Sung,
a lawyer I'd met when a Chinese gangster I'd
helped put in prison broke out and came to
town looking for revenge. The two of them hit it
off immediately, and Elizabeth gave up her
apartment in town and moved in with him.
Despite nearly forty years difference in their
ages, the two of them were totally compatible,
and inseparable. As for me, Blood was
something of a father substitute. My own dad
had been swept away, along with my mom and
aunt, in a hurricane that hit Galveston. I'd been
fortunate to have my parents through my
youth, but I found it nice to have an older
person to talk to now that I was getting a bit
long in the tooth myself.

"Man, you wasn't kiddin' when you said this
place was way out," Tucker said as we entered
the clearing.

"Safest place I can think of," I said.

Blood was standing on the front porch
watching us approach. I had no doubt that he'd
been following our journey from the time we
turned onto the dirt road. I figure he also knew
that there were two of us in the car, and had
probably started a file check to determine who
my passenger was.

I pulled up and parked a few yards from the

porch. As I got out, Blood raised his hand in greeting.

"Top of the morning to you, youngster," he said. "To what do I owe the pleasure of this early morning visit?"

He has a soft, cultured southern accent, and courtly manners. And, as usual, he was dressed for the day despite the early hour; dark dress pants, a matching dress shirt, and shined shoes.

"Morning, Blood," I said. "Sorry to drop in unannounced, but I need a favor."

"No problem, son. You know you're always welcome here anytime of the day. Who's your friend?"

His tone was mild, but there was steel in his voice. I noticed that even as we spoke, his eyes were on Tucker, sizing him up. As for Tucker, he was staring at Blood as if he was in the presence of royalty.

"M-my name's Elwood Tucker," he said. "My friends just call me Mouse, though."

"Welcome, Mr. Tucker," Raine said, looking at me. "You're one of Al's friends. I've never met you before."

I quickly and succinctly explained the relationship.

"Ah, I see," Raine said. "So, Mr. Tucker, you've run afoul of some bad people who now want you dead, right?"

"Uh, yeah; that about it; and, Mr. Pennyback here, he done promised to help me."

"And, I take it you need my assistance?" This was directed at me. "What can I do to help?"

"Well, I need to stash Tucker here for a while until I sort out the guys who're after him. I figured your place is so far off the radar he'd be safe here. Besides, even if they found out he was here, I doubt they got enough guns to take this place down."

He smiled and nodded. "You have a point there." He turned back to Tucker. "Mr. Tucker, if Al here says you're worthy of being helped, I'll take his word. You're welcome to stay here for as long as necessary, but I have a few house rules."

"Yes sir," Tucker said. "I 'preciate yo hospitality."

"It's not exactly hospitality, son," Raine said, chuckling. "You see, I have brush that needs constant trimming and cutting, and a few other chores I'm getting a little old for. If you stay here, you'll be expected to pull your weight. Oh, and one other thing; I have a lady friend who lives here with me. I catch you looking at her wrong I'll gut you like a deer and string your carcass to a tree. We clear?"

Tucker's brown face paled and his mouth dropped open. "Uh, uh, well . . ." He looked imploringly at me, but I just shrugged. "Well, okay, I guess I can live with that."

"Good. Now that we have that settled, I have a pot of fresh coffee brewing. Let's have some."

12.

After having a cup of freshly-brewed Jamaican coffee, I thanked Blood for his help and drove back home. Sandra had just finished exercising and showering as I arrived, so she went to the kitchen to fix breakfast while I did a few pushups on the bedroom floor and showered. A good night's sleep had caused her to forgive the intrusion of an unexpected guest in the wee hours of the morning, and my having exposed her lovely body to the unwelcome perusal of Elwood 'Mouse' Tucker.

Breakfast was ready and on the table by the time I'd finished showering and shaving. We ate in companionable silence, and afterwards I helped her clean the kitchen.

We decided to spend the day in – the whole day. Holiday traffic in Washington is murder, with everyone going somewhere and crowding the roads and sidewalks, especially on July 4, when people throng the Mall to watch the annual fireworks display. The temperature didn't drop until well after six, so we skipped our usual run and workout session in the barn on the heavy bag. We just sat around, sipping iced tea and listening to NPR on the radio. There wasn't much except for follow-up reports about the U.S. Justice Department snatching some Cuban kid from his relatives in Miami and returning him to his father in Cuba, and speculation that the Republicans would nominate George Bush, son of the former president, as their candidate for president when they had their national convention in Philadelphia at the end of the month.

When it got dark, we turned in early. Another quiet day on the farm.

Thursday morning, the weather did another nasty. The combination of heat and humidity caused me to break into a sweat as soon as I walked out onto my back porch, and it was only six-thirty.

I decided to skip exercising, meditating for twenty minutes instead, and then headed to the office early. River Road traffic hadn't yet picked up to rush hour levels, so it was a quiet drive. I drove with the windows open, enjoying the cool rush of morning air and listening to the dull roar of early morning planes coming for landings at Dulles Airport, just across the Potomac River from my place, and the honking of the few Canada geese that had decided against flying north for summer.

Despite my early start, Heather had still beaten me to the office.

She was sipping a fragrant tea as I walked in. There was a small container of yogurt on her desk next to her keyboard.

"Is that all you're eating for breakfast?" I asked. "That's hardly enough to keep body and soul together."

"It keeps me from having a body too large to fit in my little car, I'll have you know," she said. "And, it keeps me regular."

I winced. "I really didn't need to know that. You find anything else on O'Grady?"

"No, just more of the same. What do you plan to do about him?"

I'd been giving that some thought. If the authorities hadn't been able to pin anything on him, I was beginning to have doubts about my ability to do anything. Of course, I did have the advantage of not having to worry about his legal rights like the cops did. I wasn't planning to take him to court – what I wanted to do was take him to the cleaners.

"I thought I might pay him a visit."

Her blue eyes widened. "Are you sure that's a good idea?"

"It's the best I can come up with at the moment. Besides, I need to see him on his turf; maybe that'll give me a clue to his weakness."

"Assuming he has any, you mean."

"Yeah, that too."

"Well, just be careful. I'd hate to have to break in a new boss."

"Don't worry. I wouldn't want anyone else to have to endure watching you eat the stuff you eat."

Laughing, I went into my office, plopped into the chair behind my desk, and started fiddling with my computer. While it was making up its mind on displaying something on the screen, I looked out my window at the sliver of blue on blue I could see over the trees and between the condos, that represented the Washington Channel and a little of the Potomac River on the other side of East Potomac Park. In the far distance, I could also just get a glimpse of the

Metro and Fourteenth Street bridges that connected Northern Virginia with the District.

The computer finally beeped, indicating that it was ready. It took me a few more minutes to get onto the Internet and open my email. Not a lot there: a few ads for male organ enhancing medication, low-cost mortgages, and a solicitation for some "Who's Who in Somewhere" publication. Nothing from clients or potential clients, and no personal emails; of course, my list of friends is extremely short, so I never get personal emails anyway, and Quincy prefers talking to Heather on the phone or me in person about work. The other clients we get tend to come in over the transom, and most of them don't even own computers, so they don't send email. After a few moments of hitting the 'delete' key to clean out my account, I logged off email and turned on the computer chess game that came with the machine.

I spent the next hour futile trying to checkmate the damn computer, failing five times before giving up in disgust and turning it off. I figured the streets would be stirring around about this time, but the serious drinking wouldn't have started, so it might be a good time to pay a call on Mr. O'Grady.

It was just after nine in the morning, but the air was already beginning to feel like the inside of a sauna. Despite that, I decided to walk the three blocks to the Waterfront Metro station. I was a little sweaty by the time I boarded the Green Line train heading for Navy Yard.

The crowd on the train was the usual morning horde; a few business men in wrinkled suits heading to offices out past the Navy Yard, a group of kids, boys and girls, out of school for the summer with nothing to do but ride the subway, and a large contingent of laborers, lab technicians, and mechanics in various colors of overalls or scrubs, looking bored and ignoring each other. I squeezed into an inner-facing seat next to a portly black woman who continued to read her Bible and ignored my presence. Just as well, I didn't feel like idle chit chat. The kids got my attention; the girls with T-shirts and skirts that displayed far too much skin and the boys with their caps on backwards and baggy pants that draped off their hips, showing their shorts. They talked too loud and used language that when I was a kid would have caused the nearest adult to grab you by the ear and lecture you on proper public behavior, but in 2000, only caused the grownups within earshot to bury their heads in their newspapers or feign sleep. Times had changed; and, not for the better.

I got off at Navy Yard and immediately got caught on the escalator behind an elderly man with a butt half again as wide as mine, who decided to stand in the middle of the stair and grasp the railing on both sides, effectively creating an impassable object for all of us behind him. I could clearly hear the grumbling of those behind me, but the old man either didn't hear or didn't give a damn, because he stayed where he was until he reached the top, where he paused for a few seconds until the movement of the stairs thrust me against his back. He looked around at me, frowning, and then moved slowly away. I moved out of the way of those behind *me;* dusted myself off and headed for the exit.

The sidewalks weren't exactly crowded, but there were more people about than there'd been the last time I visited the neighborhood. No one paid particular attention to me as I made my way toward O'Grady's place. In many Washington neighborhoods, people make eye contact, even with strangers, and even say hello. But, in areas like this, everyone minded his or her own business. The only time you see people making eye contact, other than when a fight's about to start is when Johns are contracting with hookers or junkies are trying to score drugs from the street dealers.

As I approached the three-story Isle of Paradise hotel that sat next to O'Grady's headquarters, I got a sense of what its business was like. I saw two white guys in suits get out of a cab, look around furtively, and duck inside the building's front door. Out for an early morning quickie, or maybe even a drug fix. They paid me no mind, and, since they weren't my business, I didn't look too long or hard at them.

When I passed the alley between the two buildings, a space of about eight feet, I could see two beefy looking men standing around the side door into O'Grady's. I glanced at them out of the corner of my eye, and they paid me no attention. It was different, though, when I pushed through the front door of the building.

I entered a small cubicle-like space, barely big enough for the gray metal desk that sat just to the right, with muscular young black man sitting behind it. The bulge in his jacket told me he was carrying major league firepower. He looked up at me, scanned me up and down, frowning, and then said, "Sorry, bro, this here's a private club; members only."

"How does one get a membership?" I asked.

"You got to be referred by a member."

"No matter; I don't want to become a member. I'm here to see Seamus O'Grady."

His face tightened.

"What business you got with Mr. O'Grady?"

"Sorry, friend, but my message is private for him only. If you'd just tell him that my name is Al Pennyback and I'm here under a flag of truce to talk to him about Elwood Tucker, I'd appreciate it."

He looked blankly at me.

"That would be Mouse Tucker to you, probably."

His eyes widened. So, he hadn't known Tucker's real given name; no surprise I guess. I'd taken a flyer with the part about the truce flag, figuring O'Grady's fascination with the mob would extend to the old Italian courtesies. He got up and went to the door, opening it and leaning through to speak to someone on the other side. He waited a few minutes, and then nodded his head. There was a look of mild surprise on his face as he turned to face me.

"The boss'll see you, but first, I got to pat you down to make sure you ain't carryin'"

I held my arms up while he expertly frisked me for a weapon. He'd obviously been the subject of such treatment many times. Satisfied that I was unarmed, he pushed the door open and ushered me through.

His twin stood to the side of the door. He ignored me as I passed him. The place was larger inside than it looked from outside. In front of me, but about a hundred feet away, was a large mahogany bar of the kind you see in the saloons in western movies stretched halfway across the room. A bored-looking black man with a snow white afro and dressed like a bartender from the Roaring Twenties stood behind the bar polishing a glass. To the right of the bar was a staircase, and another muscled goon stood at the bottom. Next to the staircase was a large circular stage, ringed in footlights. A skinny blonde wearing what looked like three Band-Aids in strategic locations undulated in the red and yellow glow of the footlights to the beat of music coming from large speakers on the wall behind her. There were twenty or so tables scattered around; the five or six nearest the stage were occupied by men, young and middle-aged, some in workers overalls, a few in suits, leering up at the dancer. The rest of the tables had onseys and twoseys, men at some, women at others. The men; black, white, Asian, and Hispanic, about equally distributed among the twenty that I quickly counted as I crossed the room, didn't look like customers. Most had bulges under their jackets, and all watched me like a hawk watching a field mouse. The women, mostly black, with a few whites, two Hispanics and one Asian, weren't much more covered than the dancer, had on too much makeup, looked bored, and were obviously working girls.

At a table near the left end of the bar sat Seamus O'Grady. I recognized him from my previous recce, but would have known him anyway. He was white, the white of the belly of a fish, and huge. Much larger, in fact, than he appeared from across the street, and getting larger as I neared him. To his left, sat the two goons from Tucker's apartment; the larger one, Skeeter, had his right thumb in a large white cast, while the small one's left foot was in a cast. When they recognized me, angry scowls darkened their dark faces. Skeeter started to rise, but O'Grady put a huge hand on his arm.

"Now, now, Skeeter my boy," he said in an almost effeminate voice. "Mr. Pennyback is here under truce, and therefore, under my protection. You *will* treat him as a guest."

Skeeter muttered something under his breath, but sat meekly. The other one, Mo, simply glared hatred up at me.

"Won't you please have a seat, Mr. Pennyback," O'Grady said. "Can I offer you something to drink?"

"I'm fine, thanks," I said. "Is there some place we could talk in private?"

He stared at me with eyes that were buried in folds of flesh. "I suppose we could talk in my office." He inclined a massive head to his right. There was a dark, wood panel door set in the wall. Further along the wall, near the front of the room was another door, a plain wooden door, in front of which stood a massive Asian with bulging forearms.

"That might be better I said."

It wasn't just that I wanted to talk to him alone. The three of them were sitting in the only chairs facing the rest of the room, which would have left me sitting with my back not only to the door, but to all the goons in the room. The thought gave me a prickling feeling in the small of my back.

O'Grady heaved his massive bulk from the chair and waddled toward the wood panel door. He took a large gold key from the pocked of his jacket and unlocked the door, and motioned me in.

Behind the door, O'Grady lived in luxury. A huge wooden desk, all polished dark brown, sat to the right, taking up nearly a quarter of the room. A plush leather chair sat behind the desk. To the left was a large black leather sofa, two matching leather chairs, and a kidney-shaped wooden low table upon which sat a silver coffee service. The walls were paneled in a dark wood. The paintings and prints hanging on the walls looked real.

"Have a seat, Mr. Pennyback," he said, indicating one of the leather chairs. "You sure I can't offer you a cup of coffee. It's the best Turkish blend."

I'm not a great fan of the harsh Turkish coffee, but I accepted a cup to be polite.

"Now," he said, after taking a sip from his cup. "You're representing our mutual friend Mr. Tucker? What is the nature of your representation?"

I looked down at the muddy looking liquid in

my cup, and decided against drinking it.

"Mr. Tucker seems to think you've ordered him to be killed. He's asked me to intercede to get you to rescind that order."

He stared icily at me over the rim of his cup. Then, he slowly put it down on the table, and dabbed at his fleshy lips with his pudgy fingers.

"Now, why would he think such a thing?"

"Well, it could be the two goons who were trying to break into his apartment last night," I said. "In fact, the two who were sitting with you when I came in."

"Ah, you're referring to Mr. Jackson and Mr. Turner. You know, they're quite put out with you, Mr. Pennyback. They claim that you violently assaulted them when they were trying to communicate with Mr. Tucker. It's only my guarantee of your safety that kept them from doing harm to you just now."

I chuckled, which drew a frown from him.

"You think it funny?" he asked.

"Well, considering they were both armed, and I don't carry a weapon, yeah, I think it's just a bit funny. But, you didn't address my statement; will you call your goons off Tucker?"

"Mr. Pennyback, I run a rather extensive business here, and to run it successfully I must have rules and discipline. Those who violate the rules must face the consequences. To do any less would leave me vulnerable."

He spoke softly, but there was a steely menace in his voice.

"Surely, showing a little mercy from time to time wouldn't be misplaced."

"You obviously weren't raised in this kind of environment," he said. "I was, and let me tell you; down here, mercy is just another word for weak. Preachers can show mercy; for anyone else, it just marks you as a pushover. No, I'm afraid I can't help you there."

"If that's your last word, I'll pass the word along to Mr. Tucker. There's one other thing, though, I'd like to bring up; I heard a rumor that you offered to cancel Tucker's girlfriend's debt if she'd let her daughter come work for you? Is that true?"

"Not that it's any of your business, but I did offer Ms. Logan a deal. Unfortunately, she's being a bit stubborn at the moment. Why are you interested?"

I was getting tired of playing nice with this tub of bacon fat. The way he casually avoided directly answering my questions was bugging me. The way he talked about exploiting a child as if it was just another business deal made me want to smash his fat face.

"I'm interested," I said. "Because I have this thing about child prostitution; I hate it, and I don't particularly like those who deal in it. I'm politely suggesting that you back off."

He leaned forward, resting the many folds of his chin on his steepled fingers.

"Mr. Pennyback, you're not exactly in a position to *suggest* anything to me, polite or otherwise. In case you didn't notice, I have more than twenty men just outside this office. I have but to lift my protection from you, and I doubt you'd be able to handle them the way you did the two last night."

"That might be true, but you'd have a smaller work force before I went down. Besides, I figure you're a man of his word. You accepted my offer of truce. You won't break it."

"You think you're pretty smart, don't you? You're right, of course. But, the minute you walk out that front door, my protection ends. I'd watch my back if I were you."

I leaned forward, putting my hands flat on the table, and stared directly into his eyes. "If that's a threat, you need to know, I don't like being threatened."

"I don't make threats. You might consider that a friendly warning."

He laughed, the rolls of fat on his face jiggling.

I got up and walked out. Skeeter was waiting just outside the door. As I brushed past him, he placed his uninjured hand on my arm.

"You dead, nigger," he said in a low growl. "That a promise."

All eyes were on me. I could feel a tingling at the back of my neck. O'Grady had said the truce was good until I left the building, but I couldn't depend on this bunch of apes not overreacting. But, like the fat man said, down here you couldn't show weakness. Show fear and like a pack of angry dogs they'd likely pounce. I grabbed the big man's fingers and pried them from my arm, bending them back enough to cause pain. With the cast on his thumb, he couldn't use his right hand to do anything, and his friend, Mo, with the cast on his foot, couldn't move fast enough to help him. He winced in pain.

"Here's a promise for you," I said back, low enough not to be seen as challenging anyone else, but loud enough to be heard. "You come near me again, and it won't be your thumb I break next time."

I released his fingers, which he immediately stuck in his mouth, and walked slowly out the door. No one moved. Even the dancer had stopped to watch. The only sound was the dance tune that blasted from the speakers.

13.

When I got back to the office, I didn't bother telling Heather what had happened, beyond the fact that O'Grady wasn't in a mood to be forgiving. That left me with the problem of how I could change his mind. She looked skeptical at that prospect.

"Doesn't sound like the type to change his mind," she said.

"Oh, I just have to make him an offer he can't refuse," I said.

"Why does it make me nervous when you

say things like that?"

I simply shrugged and went into my office.

That's all you can do when there's nothing to say. Heather had a right to be nervous, although she couldn't have known why. I'd pretty much decided that bringing O'Grady down through legal means wasn't in the cards. Had that been possible, the system would have already taken him off the board. In order to get this rat, I'd have to get down in the rat holes of the city. It wouldn't be pretty.

I'd been sitting behind my desk, thinking about nothing in particular, for over an hour when Heather poked her head around the door. She looked pale; paler than usual; and her eyes were wide. I instantly went on alert, thinking that O'Grady or someone working for him located my office and come visiting.

"What is it, Honeybunch?" I asked.

"S-someone here to see you, boss." Her lips trembled as she spoke.

I came from behind my desk, my fists clenched; every muscle in my body tensed for action.

When I saw who was standing behind Heather, my muscles tensed even more and I felt the heat of anger in my face.

Lila Logan, her clothing dirty and torn, a

huge bruise under her left eye, and her hair askew, stood there, her shoulders slumped, and her eyes red.

"What the hell happened to you?" I asked.

"Two men come to the apartment 'bout an hour ago," she said in a trembling voice. "I locked the door like you said, but they kicked it down. They punched me 'round some, and then they took my Jeanne and left."

"Did you call the police?"

"That don't do no good. I know who done took my baby, but I ain't got no proof, and Mr. O'Grady, he got so many important people on his payroll, ain't no way the po-lice gone be listenin' to me. You the only one I could think to turn to. You got to help me get my baby back."

The anger I'd felt for O'Grady before was an eyedropper worth compared to the way I felt about him at that very moment. He'd now gone completely over the line as far as I was concerned, and I'd go just as far to make him pay.

"Why don't you sit down," I said, taking her gently by the shoulder and guiding her to the chair in front of my desk. "Heather, please get her a glass of water or tea or something." Heather ducked back into her office. "Do you need to see a doctor?"

"Naw, I'll be okay. Ain't nothin' broke. I been

beat worse in my time."

She sat, her shoulders still slumped. I stood there, at a loss as to what to do until Heather returned with a cup of hot tea and thrust it into her hands. She blew on it and took a sip.

"Is it too hot?" Heather asked.

"Naw, it's just right, thanks," she said, taking another sip.

"Where will you stay tonight?" I asked. "You can't go back to your apartment."

"I hadn't thought 'bout that. I guess I could go to one of them shelters. Be a while 'fore my landlord fix the door. I don't have the money to pay for it, either."

"She could stay at my place," Heather said.

"I'm not sure that's a good idea," I said. "I think it might be better if I imposed on Carlton Raine again. If they're both in the same place, it'll be easier to keep them safe. Besides, I'd rather you not get caught up in this."

She made a sour face. "I thought I was supposed to be on my way to becoming a full partner in this outfit? If that's the case, shouldn't I be able to carry a full load just like you?"

"Sure, but . . . hell, look at her face. These guys play rough."

She pulled herself up to her full five-six or so height and glared up at me.

"I can play rough, too, Al Pennyback; or, have you forgotten what I did to that redneck who broke in here a few years ago?"

That had been back when I was looking into the murder of one of Sandra's students. The perps, a couple of art thieves who'd killed the kid because he'd seen them with their stolen loot, broke into what they thought was an empty office to see what I'd learned. Unfortunately for them, Heather and I were in my office discussing the case and interrupted them going through her desk. She'd mangled the crotch of the guy pawing through her drawers – desk drawers – and I'd bruised the other one before they fled. Pound for pound, I'd back her against anyone in a fair fight, but O'Grady's guys weren't likely to play fair.

"These guys are likely to come after you with guns," I said.

"The locks on my doors are top of the line, and I've had reinforced doors installed front and back; I always lock my doors and never open them to strangers; and, the Arlington police answer emergency calls in my neighborhood within three minutes. If they come after her at my place, they're in for a bit of a shock."

Lila Logan's head pivoted from side to side as Heather and I talked, like a spectator at a slow ping pong match.

"Look, I don't want to be causin' nobody no trouble," she said. "I can still go to my cousin's place."

"I'm not sure that's a good idea either," I said.

"Well, what I gone do?"

"I still say she should go to my place," Heather said.

The both of them looked at me, Heather with a stubborn, determined expression, Lila just looking confused. I'd pretty much made my mind up about what my evening activities would be, and it would require a visit to Blood's place. If things worked out, Heather's place might actually be safer for her. In other words, between a mule-stubborn woman on one side, a woman depending on me for her safety on the other, and the need to get moving, I'd been maneuvered up a tree. The only way I was getting down without Heather throwing rocks at me was to give in.

"Okay, but just for tonight," I said.

They both looked relieved.

I didn't feel at all relieved.

14.

We decided to close up early, and I tailed Heather's car as far as the Fourteenth Street Bridge to make sure no one was following her. We were a few minutes ahead of rush hour, but there were still a lot of cars on the street, but I didn't notice anyone paying her car any particular attention.

I had to cross the bridge and take the George Washington Memorial Parkway to Rosslyn in order to cut across the Key Bridge into Georgetown and take Canal Road toward home. Normally that would have been a snarl, but except for the outbound traffic on the parkway, it wasn't too bad. The drive from there to River Road and my farm house took thirty minutes, which was pretty good for that time of day. The light traffic was due in large part to the fact that many of the area's workers were off on summer vacation.

Sandra was lounging on the sofa sipping lemonade when I arrived.

"Grab your hat, babe," I said. "We've got to go see Blood."

"Not that I mind, but why the rush?"

"I'll tell you when we get there," I said, taking the glass from her and finishing the cool, sweet liquid in one long swallow. I put the glass on the table and grabbed her hand. "Now, let's get moving."

She shrugged and followed me out.

"You could at least have put the dirty glass in the sink."

I usually do. I hate leaving dirty dishes lying around. But, it was important that I saw Carlton as soon as possible.

"I'll get it later."

She gave me a strange look, but didn't say anything else. She was quite, in fact, all the way to his house.

He was on the porch to greet us, a handshake for me, and a gentle peck on the cheek for Sandra.

"So nice to see your lovely face again, my dear," he said. "Elizabeth is inside, and I know she'd love to talk to you."

"Is that your way of saying you boys are up to something and you don't want me to know what it is?" she asked.

"My dear, keeping anything from you would, I believe, be nearly impossible," he said, bowing slightly. "But, Al and I do have some rather private things to discuss that I believe inappropriate for a lady's ears. Besides, you can help Elizabeth keep our house guest company."

Sandra's brows shot up. Then comprehension dawned. "Oh, yes, I forgot, you're keeping Al's client here."

"Yes, quite an engaging young man, actually; he's been quite helpful with the chores, too."

Engaging isn't exactly the word that would have first come to my mind to describe Elwood Tucker – or the second for that matter – and Sandra had a skeptical look as she mounted the steps to go inside the cabin, but Carlton wasn't one of the CIA's top agents just because he could blow things up and make people disappear; he had an innate sense of people that bordered on the uncanny.

"I'm glad he's been no trouble," I said. "But, the situation is heating up, and I think I might just have to deal with some trouble. I need your advice."

He laid a hand on my arm.

"Kind of thought you might, based on what Mouse told me," he said. "Come with me; I have something to show you."

He led me around the side of the cabin to the door of what looked like a tornado shelter. It was placed such that it could only be seen from directly in front; I'd never noticed it before; and secured with a large, steel padlock, which he opened with a brass key. I followed him down the steep steps that plunged fifteen feet into the darkness. At the bottom, he switched on a light.

Like the interior of his cabin, the space we were in was larger than it appeared from the outside. We were in an underground room twenty feet on each side, with a ten-foot ceiling, concrete floor and walls, and fluorescent lighting fixtures set into the top of the walls. A large work bench ran along the far wall. Metal cabinets that reached the ceiling lined two other walls.

"Holy crap," I said. "How long has this been here?"

"I put it in when I built the cabin," he said. "This is my workshop. I work on and store things here that I don't want to keep inside the house."

He went to the workbench and picked up a wooden box from beneath it. Reaching into the box, he pulled out a soft drink can, the top half of which was wrapped in silver duct tape. He held it up for me to see.

"Is that what I think it is?"

He chuckled as he put the can on the bench. "Well now, that kind of depends on what you think it is," he said.

"It looks suspiciously like an explosive device."

"Yes, but probably not what you're thinking. It's not designed to kill, although, if someone was fool enough to be sitting on top of it when it went off, or was holding it, I can't promise it wouldn't kill him. I've put just enough black powder in it, along with a small detonator, or in some of them a ten-second fuse, to make a big bang and a lot of smoke. I have a few that have flour in them, so they're in effect incendiaries, but again, not very big and only really dangerous if you were to put them somewhere like, say, a gas tank."

"You keep things like this around all the time?"

"No way! Far too dangerous, even small like this. But, after talking to Mouse last night, especially about this character O'Grady's moves on his girlfriend's daughter, I figured you'd be wanting to teach him a lesson, so I came out here after everyone was asleep and rigged up a few. Just enough for us to carry."

"Us?"

"Look, son; you don't think I'm planning to let you have all the fun, do you? I hate child molesters about as much as I reckon you do. Besides, you'll need someone covering your back."

I hadn't really planned for anyone else to get involved. What I was planning wasn't exactly legal, despite the fact that I'd be doing it to a piece of trash that had probably broken every law in the book. But, he was right. I was badly outnumbered, and what I was planning to do wouldn't leave me much leeway for keeping a lookout. He had a determined look on his face.

"You absolutely sure about this?" I asked.

"You think I'd go to all the trouble of making these things if I wasn't serious? Now, what's the plan?"

I told him what I planned to do. When I'd finished, he chuckled again.

"Now, that sounds like a good plan to me," he said. "I recommend we go in just after midnight. Less chance of innocent bystanders being around, and O'Grady and his goons are likely to be drowsy and not too alert."

"So, what do we do until then, boss?"

"Well, I suggest we go in the house and have some supper with the ladies – and, Mouse, of course. Then, we just relax until H-hour."

And, just like that, the plan was set into motion.

15.

Supper was nice; Blood did most of the cooking, and the man could cook. The two of us had iced tea, Tucker had a beer, and the women had white wine with golden roasted pork chops with apple sauce, chick peas, sautéed potatoes, and for dessert, apple pie with cheese.

After supper, we sat around, sipping coffee and listening to Blood tell tales of his life as a secret agent; only I knew he was leaving out the most interesting parts, mostly because much of what he did during his career was still under a top security seal; but, it had Tucker's eyes wide and his mouth agape in astonishment.

I pulled Sandra aside at one point and told her that Blood and I would be going out just before midnight, so she would be staying at his place until we got back. She's been around me long enough to know what that means, but except for a slight frown, she didn't fight it. Blood instructed Tucker to sleep on the couch and keep an eye out – not that it was necessary with all the security gizmos he had around the place, but, it kept him from asking too many questions.

Everyone but Blood and I hit the sack a little after eleven. When Tucker was snoring loudly on the couch, we tiptoed outside, retrieved the 'packages' from the shelter, along with a Luger that Blood tucked into his belt, and piled into my Mustang.

Neither of us spoke until we were two blocks away from our objective. I pulled into an alley between two warehouses, and doused the engine and the lights.

"How far is it from here?" Raine asked.

"Just a few minute walk," I said. "We can get there by way of these alleys. My plan is to go into the parking lot from the rear."

He nodded and fell in behind me, keeping an eye on our back trail as we made our way toward O'Grady's place.

The alleyway was dark, with only an occasional lance of light from street lights penetrating the gloom. I kept the pace slow to minimize the noise, cursing myself for not doing a reconnaissance beforehand to get the layout of the place. Finally, after five minutes of skulking, we passed behind the hotel, skipped quickly across the space between it and O'Grady's headquarters, and made our way around the side to the weed-strewn parking lot.

A single street lamp at the corner of the building gave enough light for us to see, but if we moved carefully, we might just not be seen – or, so I hoped. There were ten cars in the lot parked side by side away from the building, and the limo I'd seen O'Grady emerge from, parked near the front, closer to the building.

Raine came up beside me and surveyed the scene.

"Looks like some of these guys like to stay late," he said in a voice just above a whisper. "I imagine the big, fancy car near the building belongs to the boss?"

"Yeah, that's the one I saw him in. How do you want to handle this?"

He had the bombs in a canvas bag he'd hung from his shoulder. He removed one and handed it to me. It had a length of fuse protruding from the top.

"I reckon you'll want to do his car personally," he said. "I'll take care of the others. Do you have matches or a lighter?"

"I don't smoke."

"Figured as much." He handed me a Zippo lighter. "Here, use this, but wait until I give you the signal. That's a twenty second fuse; you'll have to light it and get the hell away from it fast."

"How will you light yours? Do you carry two lighters?"

He reached in the bag and pulled out a little black box with a handle on it.

"No, I plan to wire these babies to go off together. I'll use my hand crank generator here to ignite the detonators electrically." He reached in again and pulled out a small spool of wire. "Shouldn't take me more than three or four minutes to do ten cars, so you watch me. When I give you the signal, light that fuse and hightail it back to the corner of the building."

I nodded and began working my way across the lot toward the big car. I eased along the back of the area, keeping in the shadows as much as I could, until I reached the corner of the building, and then I walked along, just inches from the brick facing, until I came abreast of the vehicle. I then crouched near the right front tire and looked over toward the other side where the other cars were parked in a ragged row. Blood had already placed cans on the first two cars, and I could see him working his way from the third. The man was amazing. He moved like a shadow. Had I not known what he was up to, I might not have even been able to see him.

In short order, he'd made his way to the last car, affixed the war, and was working his way back to our starting point. He looked over toward me – I could swear that even though I was crouched in a dark shadow, he could see me as clear as day – and waved.

I crab walked toward the back tire. I sat the can on top of the tire; it just fit, leaving space for the fuse; made sure it was stable, lit the fuse, and then, bending low, ran toward the back of the building. I made it to Blood's position in about ten seconds. He was crouched in the shadows, but I could see a smile on his face.

"Think I'll wait until yours goes before I trigger mine," he said. "So, instead of one *big* boom, they'll hear two. Ought to get their attention."

Just then, there was a big *Boom!* as the charge I'd left on O'Grady's car detonated.

There was a flash first, followed by the sound, followed by a second flash/sound almost in unison as the gas in the car's tank ignited. Contrary to what you see in the movies, gasoline doesn't really explode; in fact, the liquid doesn't burn; what happens is the vapors ignite, causing more vapors, which ignite, and . . . well, you get the picture; you get a really rip-roaring fire. Blood turned the handle on his detonator, and there was an even bigger *Boom!* as the charges under the other cars detonated all at once. A couple of the tanks ignited, making three great bonfires in the parking lot. At the front of the building, over the roar of the fires, we could hear shouting and cursing. Our work had been noticed.

"Time to vacate the premises," I said.

"Think you're right, son," he said.

As we turned to go, I heard O'Grady's voice in the commotion, "Somebody get that damn car away from the building. I got important stuff inside, and I don't want the fucking building catching fire."

I could see several men with fire extinguishers, vainly spraying the big car, which was now engulfed in flames. They concentrated on the front to keep the flames from leaping to the building. A few others ran over to the other cars, most of which were merely damaged, but not burning. The curses we heard would have embarrassed a sailor.

Round one to us. We'd hit them where it hurt. Now, it was time to retreat and plan round two. We didn't waste any more time as we made our way back to my car.

16.

Raine was as close to jubilant during the ride back to his place as I'd ever seen him.

"Whew," he said. "I haven't had that much fun in years. Son, you've got to include me in more of your cases."

"They don't usually involve blowing things up," I said. "Mostly, I'm just tracking down people who don't want to be found for one reason or another."

He sat back in the seat, a satisfied look on his face.

"That's too bad. Man needs a little excitement now and then."

"Doesn't Elizabeth provide enough of that for you?"

"Not that kind of excitement, boy, not that I'm knocking it. No, I'm talking about the thrill of the hunt, the life and death excitement of going up against something that's bigger than you are, and prevailing."

"I would have thought you'd have gotten enough of that when you were active with the agency," I said.

"I don't think you can ever get enough."

I sort of knew what he was talking about. There were times when I missed going on patrol with my team, tracking down drug lords or terrorists in some godforsaken jungle or mountain hideout. My last mission, though, when faulty intelligence caused us to wipe out a warlord's entire family because the pukes in the intel shop hadn't bothered to tell us they were with him, soured me on the whole business. That mission, one in which I'd shot a young girl to death – notwithstanding the fact that she had an AK, and would have gladly shot me – was the reason I didn't carry a gun. If I can't handle it with my fists or feet, or talk my way out of it, I just run like hell in the opposite direction.

"There *is* one other little task I might need your help with," I said.

"Name it, son."

"Tucker's girlfriend, Lila Logan; you remember, I told you about her?" He nodded. "Well, O'Grady's thugs snatched her. I aim to get her back."

"You can count me in, but we need to find out where they're holding her."

"I think I know where," I said. "I think he's holding her right under our noses – there in his building."

"So, we just have to get in without being seen, get the girl, and get out without getting our hind ends shot off."

"Yeah, something like that."

"Piece of cake. We can plan the operation when we get back to my place. By the way, I think you should make my place your base of operations until we neutralize these guys. Won't take long for them to figure out you were behind tonight's mischief, and if they come looking for you, your place is not too secure. And, you definitely don't want to leave that lady of yours there by herself."

I hadn't thought about that possibility. Now, in addition to having to figure out how to rescue Jeanne Logan, I had to come up with a way to tell Sandra that she was going to be Carlton Raine's house guest for an indeterminate time.

Things just kept getting better and better.

17.

When we got back to the house, convincing Sandra didn't turn out to be as difficult as I'd feared. When we entered the living room, the noise of the door opening woke Tucker. When we told him what we'd done, he jumped up and ran around the room, punching the air with his fist and shouting 'yay,' which woke Sandra and Elizabeth. They came out in their robes to see what the commotion was, and Tucker filled them in. They just walked over and sat on the sofa and looked at us with their eyes wide.

Finally, Elizabeth broke the silence.

"You two are like little boys. You're always looking for something to break or blow up."

"I suppose you're going back tonight to rescue the girl?" Sandra asked.

"Got to," Raine said. "If they have her in that building, we can't be sure they'll keep her there.

The longer we wait, the more chance they'll move her."

"Can I go with you this time?" Tucker asked.

"No, son," Raine said before I could speak. "This is an operation that requires special skills. Al and I have those skills, and you don't. Nothing personal, you understand, and you're a good man for offering, but you're still better off here guarding the women." He ducked his head and smiled shyly at Sandra and Elizabeth as he said that. They just made sniffing noises.

Then, I heard a beeping sound.

"Wha. . ."

"Got company coming," Raine said, interrupting me. "That alarm signals they just turned off River Road."

"I don't want to sound alarmist, but are we prepared for an attack?"

"Don't you worry yourself, son," he said. "The rest of you folk just make yourselves comfortable here in the parlor. Elizabeth, honey, you mind making a pot of coffee for our guests, since I don't think anyone will be going back to sleep right away." She smiled and went into the kitchen. "Now, Al, if you'll come with me, I'll show you how I deal with uninvited guests."

He led me to the room in the back of the . . .

parlor . . ., the one with the reinforced door that was always locked. Here, I knew, was his monitoring station, but I'd never really seen it in operation. He unlocked the door and ushered me inside, closing it firmly behind him. There were two chairs in front of the drop front desk. Above the desk was a three-door cabinet. He sat in the chair in front of the computer terminal, motioning me to the other. Reaching up, he opened the center cabinet door. In the cabinet was a large monitor, or TV set, I couldn't tell which. On it was a schematic of the area, with the cabin in the middle. The roads were marked in brown, and there were concentric circles radiating out from the cabin. Four red dots were moving slowly along the brown line representing the road.

"Does each of those dots represent a car?" I asked.

"Yup, and assuming four people in each vehicle, that means we have sixteen bad guys incoming."

"Shit, Blood, how are we gonna cope with that many armed guys?"

The dots were approaching the second line from the outer perimeter.

"Just watch, son. I'm going to send them a polite warning to turn around when they hit that line."

He put his fingers on the computer keyboard. The monitor lighted up, showing a chart that had three sections, blue, orange, and red. He tapped the keys, and the blue section lit up.

As the first dot approached the line on the map, he tapped a key. The big screen flickered, and the dots stopped.

"That was a couple of small explosions off to the side of the road. They're accompanied by a recorded message telling them they're trespassing, and to turn around and go back to River Road. If they ignore that, my orange line methods are a bit harsher."

"Does this happen often?"

"Once or twice a year. Usually it's someone who accidentally took a wrong turn. When they hear that message, they immediately realize their mistake and turn around pretty fast and leave. I've never had anyone pass the blue line." The red dots resumed their forward movement. "Until now, that is. Okay, I guess they want to play tough."

A few more taps of the keys and the blue section on the monitor went dark. The orange section lit up.

"Why don't you have labels on there to tell you what's gonna happen?"

"Don't need it. I put the system in; I know

what's there. No one else needs to know."

"What happens at the orange line?"

"I have a couple of automatic rifles mounted in the trees. I can control them from here." He did something with the computer, and an eerie green on black picture on the screen replaced the graph. It showed the four cars moving slowly along the dirt road, kicking up dust as they moved. A few more key strokes and the picture zoomed in on the lead car. In the green glow I could see a large dark face behind the wheel, and a lighter skinned one in the passenger side. The two in the back seat were in shadow.

Raine kept moving his gaze from the video on the computer screen to the graphic map in the cabinet. When the lead dot was almost touching the red line representing the third circle, he began tapping the keys more quickly. The picture zoomed in even closer and dipped down until only the front grille of the car was showing. Then, the picture jerked slightly, and the car stopped moving. There were three round holes in the grille. Raine reached behind the computer and pulled a small microphone out. When he spoke into it, the tone in his voice sent chills through me.

"Gentlemen," he said slowly. "That's the last warning shot. If you go a foot further, the next shots will be at your heads. Just in case you think I'm joking, watch what happens to your rear view mirror." He did some more typing and the picture zoomed in on the chrome mirror affixed to the driver's side. A tap on the keyboard and the mirror flew apart as three high-powered rounds slammed into it. "Now, your heads are somewhat larger than that mirror, and a damn sight easier to hit. I hope I've made myself clear. Oh, and should any of you be fast enough and lucky enough to get past this point, I can assure you that you won't survive what will be waiting for you."

Whether it was the tone of his voice, or the shots so accurately placed from some unseen location, I don't know, but the cars began backing up and trying to make three-point turns on the narrow road. After a bit of backing and forthing, they finally got turned around and headed toward River Road, kicking up so much dust, they were lost to view.

"What would have happened to the ones who got past that point?" I asked.

"You don't really want to know," he said. "Besides; just sixteen of them; it's hardly likely they would have. If I'd taken out the first car, the others would have been blocked in. Trying to drive off the road's a bad idea; some really bad things can happen to your tires. And, walking's even worse. I got Malayan gates, punji pits, and a few other nice surprises out there in those woods."

"Remind me never to go walking around your place."

"Not without me as a guide, for sure it wouldn't be a good idea. Well, let's go out and have coffee with the ladies."

At about three, we finally felt tired enough to go back to sleep. It turned out that the cabin had two bedrooms, so Sandra and I took the spare, leaving Tucker on the sofa. I fell asleep as soon as I lay down.

Three hours later, my eyes snapped open. There was the tiniest sliver of light coming through the center of the curtains where they didn't quite meet; just enough to wake me. I started to roll out of bed for my morning run, when I remembered where I was. I didn't like the idea of *not* exercising, though, so I got up anyway and padded barefoot through the living room to the front porch. I did crunches, pushups, and knee bends on the rough wooden boards until I'd worked up a good sweat, and then I sat cross legged and meditated for fifteen minutes staring at the trees in front of the cabin.

I was just coming out of my relaxed meditative state when I heard Carlton Raine's cultured southern accent behind me.

"I see you like to get up early and start the

day with exercise, too," he said. "I find it gets my blood pumping better and gives me a better appetite. I meditate, too. Works wonders for the blood pressure."

I stood up and stretched. "If I'd known, I would've waited for you."

"No need. I do mine in the bedroom, quietly so I don't wake Elizabeth up. You ready for some breakfast?"

"Yeah, but I need to shower first," I said.

Despite the two bedrooms, the cabin only had one bath. Blood, ever the southern gentleman, let me go first. After we'd both cleaned up, I joined him in the kitchen as he prepared breakfast. Like me, he'd grown up eating substantial breakfasts, and believed that the day didn't start properly until one had eaten properly. He made *huevos rancheros*, with an extra handful of *jalapenos* like I like, biscuits with a dot of cheese on top, thick ham slices fried golden brown, and hash brown potatoes with fresh chopped garlic.

He had me grind some Jamaican coffee beans and start a fresh pot of coffee.

The smell of food cooking roused the others, and one by one they got themselves presentable and joined us around the wooden table that took up a lot of the kitchen's floor space. To my surprise, Blood also had a good supply of buttermilk. I've loved the stuff since I was a kid, but not many stores carry it anymore, reasoning that few people drink it, and prefer yogurt instead. Not only do I like drinking buttermilk – which grosses Sandra out – but, it's great for cooking. Fortunately for me as an army retiree I have access to the commissary at the Fort Myer army base in Arlington, and it always has a good supply.

As we sat around the table devouring Blood's sumptuous breakfast, Blood and I with coffee and buttermilk, everyone else with coffee and orange juice, there was little conversation. Whoever came up with the idea of dinner table conversation must have grown up in a household where the food was lousy. When you're sitting around a table laden with good food, the thing uppermost in your mind is *eating* it. Conversation can wait until the food's finished.

After we finished eating Sandra and Elizabeth volunteered to clean the kitchen. Blood, Tucker and I took our coffee to the parlor. I was just about to discuss the plans to rescue Jeanne Logan when my phone rang. I looked at the little display screen. It was a 202 area code, but I didn't recognize the number.

"Al Pennyback here," I said.

"Mr. Pennyback," a high, nasally voice said. "So nice to talk to you this fine morning."

Then I recognized the voice – it was O'Grady.

"What do you want?" I asked.

"Oh, I think you know what I want, Mr. Pennyback. But, what's more important is what *you* want. One of my boys saw you and your friend last night when our cars were torched. I must say, that's quite a place he has. If I had such defenses you would never have been able to do what you did."

"Look, O'Grady; could you get to the point?"

"Such impatience, my friend. You really need to learn to relax. I know you want the Logan girl – although, I don't know why you bother. I'd be willing to trade her, though, for Mr. Tucker."

"No deal."

"Now, I had a feeling you might say that. I have a sweetener, though. They say that every man has his price. Somehow, I don't think your price is measured in dollars, Mr. Pennyback. How about this? Would you be willing to trade Tucker for your assistant, the scrappy Ms. Bunche, Lila Logan, and the girl?"

"What the hell are you talking about?"

"Just what I said. Since my boys couldn't get at you, we went for the next best thing. Got her as she was taking out the garbage; can you imagine that? She gave them quite a fight, that girl did. Oh, don't worry; I respect a fighter, and she hasn't been hurt – yet. You have until noon, though, to make up your mind."

Then, he broke the connection. My face felt hot, and my emotions must have been apparent.

"What is it?" Raine asked.

I told him.

"Damn it," he said. "Now, they've really crossed the line. We can't waste any time if we're going to rescue all three of them before the noon deadline."

"I should really call Buster," I said.

"You could do that, son. Buster's a good man; I have the utmost respect for him. But, he's a cop, and he has to follow the rules. Following the rules right now could get that sweet little Heather killed, and I for one don't intend to let that happen."

"Okay, so we call Buster after we rescue them. Any ideas on how to do that?"

"Well, I'm guessing O'Grady will want to keep them close, so they'll be somewhere in his building. Last night, I noticed that building next door, a hotel is it; it's a couple of floors higher, so we ought to be able to go in from his roof if we access it from there, don't you think?"

It must be true what they say; great minds

do think alike. That had been my first thought. Of course, that meant getting into the hotel without attracting attention. We huddled to come up with a way to do that.

18.

According to the theory of Occam's razor, named for the medieval philosopher William of Occam, when you're faced with a problem that has multiple possible solutions, the simplest solution is probably correct.

Taking that into account, Blood and I decided against a complex assault on O'Grady and his thugs. We wouldn't be expected to hit them directly. So, we'd hit them directly. They wouldn't expect us to hit them from above. We planned to get onto the roof of the building from the adjacent hotel, and do just that – after we rescued the girls, of course.

Tucker argued again to be included. Blood was still against it, but when the little man made his proposal, it made sense to me. He would round up friends from his neighborhood; people not employed by O'Grady, and use them to create a distraction in front of the place while

Blood and I went in through the upper floor. It made sense, and it would mean he was close where I could better protect him. Blood finally relented and agreed that he could participate. I was beginning to change my mind about him, and I could see a grudging respect for him in Blood's eyes as well. If he was willing to put himself on the line for someone else, he couldn't be all bad.

With Tucker settled, Blood and I went back to his control room where he began the process of assembling the equipment he thought we'd need. First was a hundred feet of 11.3mm nylon climbing rope, which he had looped in a neat five-pound bundle. He put the rope inside a black canvas bag that he pulled from beneath the counter to the left of his computer desk. He then selected four carabiners, the metal D-rings climbers use to hook things to ropes. His, though, were different; they had little round, doughnut-shaped devices attached to the bottom of the D.

"Makes them into very effective pulleys," he said when he saw me looking curiously." He picked up a rope contraption that he identified as a 'seat,' which would be hooked to the D-ring to serve as transport for a person from one location to another. "Sort of a slide for life. We'll have to move fast, because we won't be able to do more than one person at a time."

I nodded; my . . . our plan would depend in

part on Tucker and his crowd keeping a large number of O'Grady's thugs distracted, and in part on my being able to find the three kidnap victims and get them to a single egress point before being spotted. It was the simplest plan we could come up with. My eyes widened when Blood pulled what looked like a .45 from the desk drawer.

"Do you think we'll need firepower like that? We'll be in pretty close quarters. Good chance any shooting starts, innocent people might get hit."

"No problem with this," he said. He reached into the drawer and withdrew a box containing six darts nestled in foam cushions. "This won't kill anyone; just put them to sleep." He tucked the gun into his belt and pulled his shirt over it. I'd never seen him with his shirt out before – it made him look even more dangerous.

"I didn't think you were supposed to use tranquilizer guns on humans. Isn't it dangerous?"

"Well, you do have people who believe that. It's not true, though. The agency's tested these babies, and the dose of Diazepam, which is basically just valium, in each dart will cause torpor and disorientation in a 180-pound man in less than a minute. It might be dangerous for a small person or a child, but I don't plan on using it on women and children. This just might give us the edge we need; especially when we go into that hotel."

I trusted Blood's judgment. He had much more experience with stuff like this than I did, and if he said the agency had given it a seal of approval, that was good enough for me.

After Blood had put the tranquilizer darts into the bag, we said goodbye to Sandra and Elizabeth and took it outside and piled into my Mustang; Tucker in the back seat with the bag, and Blood riding shotgun. I made a quick stop at my place to get my K-bar knife, which I put in a sheath strapped to my right ankle, and then we were off to battle.

19.

We pulled into an alley two blocks from the Isle of Paradise Hotel about an hour later. I took the bag out of the back seat and slung it over my shoulder.

"I could carry that, Al," Blood said.

"No problem; you need to be thinking about what we'll do once we're inside the hotel."

He gave me a skeptical look, and then shrugged. He reached into the bag and withdrew the box of darts. Removing one, he replaced the box and removed the gun from his belt and inserted the dart.

"I'll just play it by ear," he said.

I turned to Tucker. "You know what you have to do?"

"Sure," he said. "I go round up some of my home boys and we make a ruckus in front of O'Grady's building. Give me about ten or fifteen minutes."

I looked at Blood who nodded. "That should give us enough time to get to the roof," he said.

Tucker scurried off.

With Blood following, I walked out to the sidewalk and headed toward the hotel. It was just after eight-thirty, and except for a few laborers heading to work there weren't too many people about. The sidewalk in front of the Isle of Paradise was empty except for a few empty whisky bottles scattered near the wall.

We walked up the age and soot-darkened marble steps and into the lobby. The desk, behind which sat a middle-aged black man with a receding hairline, was to the immediate right. To the left were a ratty looking sofa and two chairs around a large wooden table. Some crumpled newspapers lay scattered on the table. To the rear was what looked like a combination dining room and bar that appeared not to have been used lately if the dust on the floor and every other horizontal surface was any indication. The walls were a dark green with lighter green lines at regular intervals. There were no pictures on the walls. At one time, it was probably a nice little hotel for business people visiting the area, but it had seen better days.

As we approached the desk, the clerk looked up and smiled. His teeth were crooked and brown.

"Can I help you gents?" he asked in a bored voice.

Blood moved up beside me and smiled broadly at him.

"We'd like to go up to your roof," he said.

"It's a little early . . . uh, why you want to go to the roof?" the clerk asked. "Ain't nothin' up there. Couldn't I interest you gents in some early morning entertainment? Rooms go for twenty dollar an hour; entertainment's extra and between you and the entertainer, if you get my drift. If you don't mind waitin' a few minutes, I can get two here for you."

"No," Blood said. "We want to go to the roof."

"Well, I don't rightly know I can let you do that."

"That's too bad," Blood said, and pulled the tranquilizer gun from his belt and shot the clerk in the center of his chest.

The man made a strangling sound and his eyes bugged out. He looked down at the .50 caliber dart stuck in his chest with a puzzled look on his face. His eyes then lost focus and he started to drool and sank down behind the counter.

"Put the bag over there and help me move him," Blood said.

"How long will he be out?"

"At least an hour, maybe longer."

"He didn't look too good when that stuff hit him," I said. "You sure it won't kill him?"

"Well, I'm not a hundred percent sure. If he doesn't have heart problems, he should come around okay. Too late to worry about it now."

I put the bag down in front of the counter and we hauled the comatose clerk over to a door set in the wall a few feet away. It was a janitorial closet containing mops, brooms, and large buckets. Like the dining room, it looked like it hadn't been used much. We put him in the closet, lying his side so he wouldn't choke on his drool, and shut the door.

Retrieving the bag, I led the way up the stairs to the third floor. The door to the roof was locked, but a hard kick took care of that.

The roof was flat and had the elevator housing which made creaking sounds, and a large industrial air conditioning unit set on metal struts. I put the bag down near the air unit and walked to the edge of the roof. I could see the roof of O'Grady's building, a floor below and eight feet across from us. It was similar to the hotel roof except for the absence of an elevator housing. Looking down, I saw the two men at the door near the front of the building squatting down against the wall playing dice.

Blood removed the rope and gear from the bag and began attaching it with pulleys to the struts of the a/c unit. I kept watch below.

Suddenly, as if someone had flipped on a radio, noise erupted from in front of the building next door. The dice players stopped what they were doing and rushed to the corner, peering around it. I could see them looking at each other with perplexed expressions and shaking their heads.

Tucker had apparently come through with the distraction he'd promised. It was now on our shoulders – and my legs. I walked back from the edge of the roof, looked over at Blood, who nodded, took a deep breath, and started running back toward it. I was going at a pretty good clip when I raised my left leg, planting my left foot on the little hip wall, followed up by bringing up my right foot and throwing it forward, launching myself into the eight foot space between the buildings. Eight feet might not seem like much, but broad jumping wasn't my sport in high school, and when there's a three-story drop if you miss your target, well . . . it gets the adrenaline pumping.

That surge of fear-induced adrenaline, though, probably helped. I passed over the edge of the building in my downward trajectory, hitting the surface about three feet past – an eleven foot broad jump; a record for me. I hit with my feet together and my knees bent, and immediately went into a rolling fall as if I'd parachuted onto the roof, sending the loose gravel flying in a cloud of the stinging pebbles. In the process, I scratched my right arm, and felt like I'd bruised my right buttock, but I wasn't bleeding, and when I stood, I didn't feel any sharp pains. In fact, except for the burning sensation on my right forearm and a dull pain in my butt, I felt kind of elated. I walked to the roof edge and waved up at Blood, who was standing there giving me two thumbs up and smiling as if he'd been the one to make the jump.

He took the rope and tackle, whirled it cowboy style, and tossed it at me. The metal pulley missed my head by inches. I grabbed the rope and pulled it in.

I attached the rope and pulley assembly to the frame of the air conditioner unit stand, an almost duplicate of the one on the hotel roof. The rope made a continuous loop through my pulley and the one Blood had rigged up. The nylon rope would hold up to 200 pounds without any strain, and I only hoped the metal struts were solidly anchored.

When I was satisfied that I'd tied all the knots the way Blood had instructed, I went in search of the roof access door. It was on the far side of the roof, in the rear, set in an outhouse-like building. I pulled on it, knowing that, like most such doors it would open outward, but it wouldn't budge. So, I tried pushing, but that didn't work either. It was locked. It took me all of fifteen seconds with my K-bar to remedy that. I only hoped that no one on the floor below had heard the noise.

20.

The antechamber at the top of the stairs not only looked like an outhouse, it *smelled* like one. Someone had been taking a leak in the corner, from the eye-stinging ammonia-like odor in the fetid air. I quickly made my way to the landing of the second floor, a long narrow hallway that ran the width of the building, transected by a back to front hallway. There were eight doors in the hallway, three adjacent to the stair landing and five opposite, two at the far end beyond the perpendicular hall. All the doors were open, and from the noise coming from the level below, I guessed the occupants had all gone down to see what was happening.

I could hear shouting; clear from downstairs, and muffled from outside. O'Grady's voice rose above the din.

"Get them fuckers away from the building this instant!"

"But, boss," a squeaky voice responded. "They's more of them than us."

"Do any of them have guns?"

"Then get a few pieces," O'Grady said. "That should even the odds."

"You want we should shoot a few of them, boss?"

"Only if you have to. After all, most of them are regular customers. Now, get them out of here. It's bad for business."

I heard the sound of hard soles running across the floor.

"Get some pieces, boys. Let's make the homeys run."

There was laughter and the sound of chairs scraping against the floor.

They seemed fully occupied with Tucker's little diversion. I made a quick check of the eight rooms on the hallway, confirming that they were empty, and moved down the narrow hall toward the front of the building. There were two more cross hallways, with six doors to my left and four to my right. The doors on the left were closed, but I saw no sign of locks. The four on my right all had hasps and large padlocks. I turned left.

I tried the first door on my left. It wasn't

locked. I pushed it open.

"Hello, hon," a cracked voice said. "Why ain't you downstairs with the others?"

The voice came from a woman sitting on the rumpled bed. She was almost dressed in a filmy thing that draped over her bony shoulders and gave me more of a view of her droopy breasts than I wanted or needed to see. Her face had more lines than a wrinkled roadmap, and the heavy application of dark eye shadow didn't help. Her lank blonde hair looked like it could use a shampoo.

"I could ask you the same thing." I said.

She laughed. It sounded like the old crone in *The Wizard of Oz*, the original version. "Sadie don't need to be no where people might start throwin' things. No, I plan to wait right here until things quiet down and the clients come back. The way you lookin' 'round, I take it you ain't no client?"

You don't get old without learning a few things.

"Not exactly; I'm looking for someone, well, three someones as a matter of fact; a girl and two women. You happen to see them around lately?"

"Maybe, maybe not. What's it worth to you?"

I don't usually carry large sums of cash

around with me. I had three tens and four twenties in my wallet. I took a wild guess that Sadie wasn't one of the top-of-the-line hookers in O'Grady's stable, and took out the three tens and waved them in front of her face. Her faded blue eyes tracked the crinkled bills like a cat watching a canary.

"Will this open the information flood gates?" I asked.

"I usually get fifty from my customers," she said, ducking her head coyly and gazing up at me through scraggly lashes. "Ought to be worth that at least."

Shit, I thought; I don't pay for sex, and I hate paying for information. But, I didn't have time to stand around dickering. I took a twenty out and waved it. "Okay, fifty it is; but, I pay *after* delivery."

She snatched the money from my hand. "Well, baby, I get paid up front, just like a fast food joint." When I leaned forward frowning, she held up a liver-spotted hand. "But, don't worry, Sadie don't cheat. I give value for money. The ones you're looking for are just down the hall, same side's my room. They got a cute girl they brought in the day before, and two women, one black, one white, they brought in early this morning. The white chick is a feisty little blonde, near took one of the guy's ear off when they was tryin' to lock her in, kept kicking and punching to beat the band."

"Did they look like they'd been hurt?" That would add to the list of things O'Grady would have to pay for.

"No, not really. The black chick had some bruises, but they looked old. They was just rumpled, and mad as hell."

"Okay, Sadie, thanks for the information." I saluted her and left.

"Sure you don't want a little extra, hon?" she called to my parting back.

I ignored her invitation and walked across to the first locked door. The lock was tempered steel, but the hasp was secured to the door with plain screws. It took me a minute, using my knife, to pry it from the wall. Then, a sharp kick near the knob splintered the door and frame, sending it swinging inward.

Jeanne Logan sat on a bed at the far side of the room, hugging her knees which were up to her chin. Her eyes were wide with fear.

"Hi, Jeanne; remember me?" I said. "I'm a friend of your mother's, and I'm here to take you home."

She bolted off the bed and wrapped her thin arms around my waist, sobbing. Gently, I pried her arms loose.

"I heard my momma a little while ago," she said between sobs. "You know where she is? We got to get her, too."

"Don't worry, sweetheart. We'll get your mother too. Now, stay close to me."

I led her out of the room and went to the next door. I repeated the action with the hasp and kicked that door in as well. Heather, a fierce look on her elfin face, and Lila, looking dejected, sat on the bed. Their eyes went wide when they saw me.

"Boss," Heather said. "I knew you'd come. See, Lila; didn't I tell you he'd come for us."

Lila Logan wasn't paying any attention. When she saw her daughter, she leapt off the bed and swept the girl into her arms. "Oh, my baby," she said. "I was so worried 'bout you. You okay? Did they hurt you?"

"Naw, momma," the girl said. "I'm okay. They just kept me locked in that room. Wouldn't even let me go to the bathroom. I had to pee in a coffee can. It was so gross."

"Okay, ladies," I said. "Time for reunions later. We've got to get out of here."

"How are we going to get past all those goons downstairs?" Heather asked.

"We're going out via the roof, Honeybunch; now, let's go."

"What about the other two girls?" Jeanne asked.

"What other two girls?" I asked.

"Well, when they brought me here, there was two girls I saw. They in them rooms." She pointed to the two rooms facing us. "They looked so scared. Momma, we can't just go and leave 'em."

Lila Logan looked from her daughter to me, her eyes pleading.

"Okay," I said. "Let's take a look."

I walked over and rapped on the door opposite the room Jeanne Logan had been in. A tiny voice answered, "W-who is it?"

"Friends, come to get you out of here," I said. "Stand back from the door."

Using my knife, I pried the hasp from the door frame and kicked the door in. A small girl with red hair and a face full of freckles, no more than five feet high, but dressed like a trollop, stood in the middle of the room staring goggle-eyed at me. I grabbed her arm and pulled her toward Heather. I then went to the other door and repeated my routine of removing the hasp and smashing the door with my foot. The girl in this room was even smaller; dark brown skin with her black hair done in neat cornrows. She looked equally frightened, and pulled back at first when I took her arm. Lila Logan came in and comforted her.

"Okay, everyone; follow me to the roof," I said.

As we made our way to the roof access door, I noticed the old whore, Sadie, standing in the door to her room, looking at our strange procession through narrowed eyes.

"You sure you don't want to go with us?" I said. "This place could get pretty hot soon."

She shook her head.

"Naw; think I'll just stay here," she said.

If I hadn't been so preoccupied with getting Heather and the others out of there before O'Grady's goons discovered my presence, I might have picked up on the tension in her voice, or the glimmer in her rheumy blue eyes. The volume of the noise from downstairs, and the muted roar of the crowd outside had all increased. Apparently, thugs with guns hadn't caused the crowd to disperse. Considering mob psychology, the appearance of guns, before someone is actually shot, is more likely to further inflame a crowd than cow it. Even if someone is shot, it's hard to predict how a crowd will react. O'Grady and his crew were getting a lesson in crowd control the hard way.

But, I turned my attention back to my primary objective; getting my charges safely away. I led them to the door and stood watch as they filed up the stairs. When Heather, who was bringing up the rear, passed me, I entered the stairwell and pulled the door closed.

I followed her to the roof, where the others were milling around in front of the door.

"Over by the air conditioner," I said.

Everyone followed me. When she saw the rope and pulley rig, Heather turned on me. "You're not planning for us to ride in that thing, are you?"

"Trust me, Heather, that rope will hold a lot more than your weight."

She nodded, but still looked skeptical. "If it's okay with you, I'll go last," she said.

"Actually, I'll be going last," I said. "After I've gotten the five of you off."

"How are you going to do that? I mean, you'll be here. What will we do when we get to the other side?"

I pointed to the roof of the hotel. Blood peered over the edge and waved.

"Oh," she said. "You didn't tell me you had that nice Mr. Raine helping you. That's a different story." She turned to the others. "Okay, guys, we're getting out of here."

21.

After I explained how things would work, it was decided to send Jeanne over first. She was larger than either of the other two girls, and to minimize the time it would take, I'd proposed sending them over together with the women, Heather taking the black girl who was the larger of the two, and sending the redhead with Lila.

The rig they would ride in was relatively simple; a cinch around their waist and two loops through which they put their legs. Blood had come up with it, so I felt sure it would work. It was secured to the pulley rope near the join, and once the person was inside, Blood would pull her over from his side, get her out, and send the rig back.

Jeanne's face had a stricken look when I settled her in the harness.

"Don't you worry, sweetheart," I said. "You just hang tight to the rope here, and squeeze your eyes shut so you won't be bothered by the height. You'll be over on the other roof before you know. The gentleman on the other side is a friend of mine, so don't be afraid of him, okay?"

She nodded and closed her eyes, clenching them so tight it made little wrinkles at the corners. And, she hugged that rope like a long lost lover.

I waved at Blood who began to pull the rope. I held the girl steady until she was free of the ledge and then watched her progress as she was pulled across the eight-foot space between the buildings. The whole trip, until she was taken from the harness at the other end, took thirty seconds.

Looking down, I could see the two guards in the alley still distracted by the increasingly loud crowd in front of the building.

The returning harness bumped my arm. "Okay, Ms. Logan, you and the little girl step up here. Time to go for a ride."

Logan still looked skeptical, but the little redhead, seeing how easily the first girl had made the trip, looked excited.

She put her hand on Logan's arm. "It looks like fun," she said.

Logan took a deep breath and stepped into the harness. I settled the redhead girl on her lap, facing out, and used the loose end of the harness to secure her to Logan's body. I then helped them up on the ledge and eased them off. Blood began pulling and they started across. Lila Logan's eyes were clenched shut, but the little redhead was looking around, an ecstatic smile on her freckled face.

They were almost across when I heard the door to the roof slam open, and Skeeter's squeaky voice, "That fucker must be up here some place. Way Sadie described him, can't be nobody else."

"He's probably over there," Mo, his small sidekick said. "You go 'round to the right, and I'll go left."

These two didn't get any marks for intelligence. Slamming the door, talking loud, and the way their feet scrapped over the loose gravel, I would have to have been stone deaf not to hear.

"Keep quiet, you two," I said quietly to Heather and the little girl who was clinging to her waist. "I'll take care of these two, and then get you across."

Heather nodded; a steely look in her blue eyes. "Go get 'em, boss," she whispered.

I moved right and peered around the edge of the air conditioner unit. Skeeter, his thumb still encased in a large white bandage, and with a .38 caliber police special engulfed in his other hand, was moving toward me. He further showed his lack of intelligence by not taking into account that his pal, Mo, was dragging his foot, unable to keep pace with his big friend. I ducked back and waited.

Moments later, the black barrel of the .38 poked around the corner, followed by Skeeter's hand and arm. I reached down with my left hand and grabbed his thumb. Using my own thumb for leverage, I bent his thumb back sharply. There was s sound like a dry Popsicle stick breaking. His fingers splayed and the .38 fell to the roof. He opened his mouth to scream, but before a sound could come out, I slammed my right fist into his temple. He slumped forward.

I caught him before he could fall all the way, and drug his body around in front of the a/c unit. I then walked back the way he'd come until I reached the corner. Peering around it I saw that Mo's foot had caused him to drop way behind. He was carrying a sawed off shotgun, and wincing every time he moved his bandage-encased foot. His attention was focused on the direction he was heading instead of watching for his friend. As he got within ten feet, I pulled the dart gun from my belt, stepped out, adopted a shooting stance, and shot him in the neck. The force of the dart, propelled by a blast of air from the gun, caused him to step back and reach for the pain in his neck. In doing so, his attention was diverted from his goal and the gun in his hand, and his eyes were already beginning to glaze over as the powerful tranquilizer coursed through his body.

Moving fast, I darted to him and snatched the shotgun from his limp grip with my right hand, and hit him on the point of the chin with my left. He stiffened and fell over backwards. He didn't move.

I then ran back to the roof edge, and, putting the shotgun down, helped Heather into the harness, which Blood had returned to my side while I was fighting off Skeeter and Mo. When Heather was in snugly, holding on to the frightened little girl, I signaled Blood to begin hauling them across.

As they pulled away from the ledge, I heard a noise below. Looking down, I saw that one of the guards had returned to the door. He was looking up at Heather and gesturing. He then began to pull his weapon from his belt. I quickly inserted a fresh dart into the dart gun and, leaning over the edge of the roof, I took quick aim and squeezed the trigger. The dart's downward trajectory took it into his shoulder, right at the junction of his neck, and it had to hurt, because he dropped his gun and grabbed at his shoulder and neck with both hands. I must have gotten lucky and hit a blood vessel, because the chemical took almost immediate effect. He looked up at the sky, his eyes rolling back, and sank to his knees, and then toppled forward to lie on his face.

By now, Heather was almost halfway across the gap. Blood had to be tired. This was his third haul without a break. I know I was getting tired, and I hadn't been pulling on the damn rope. Just as I reached up to help him, I saw that the second gunman had noticed his buddy on the ground, and was running back to him. He then looked up and saw Heather and the girl almost to the hotel roof's edge. When he began drawing his gun, I knew I wouldn't have time to put in another dart and get a good firing angle on him before he'd be able to get off a shot.

I looked around for something to distract him. Looking down, I saw I had two options; the shotgun I'd taken from the still unconscious Mo, or the still sleeping Skeeter. I moved faster than I have in a long time. Lifting Skeeter by the armpits, I drug his limp body to the edge of the roof, balancing it on the ledge. When the guard was below me and just about to steady his aim on Heather, who was now reaching for Blood's outstretched hands, I heaved Skeeter over the edge. At the same time, I yelled, "Hey, stupid; better look up!"

People seldom look up unless something catches their attention. Someone yelling at you from overhead will do it. The gunman paused and looked up at me. Another thing that will get your attention is a large, heavy object falling out of the sky toward you. Skeeter probably weighed two-forty, and he must have looked like a large refrigerator with legs as his body plummeted downward, quickly reaching terminal velocity, directly upon the gunman, who was transfixed.

Skeeter's body hit the gunman with a satisfying thud, sending the man crashing to the alley, his arms and legs outspread. From the roof, it looked like Skeeter had grown extra limbs. Neither of them would be going anywhere for a while.

I turned my attention back to the rope. Heather was now on the hotel roof, handing the girl to Blood. I breathed a sigh of relief. Now, all I had to do was get myself across. I began untying the rope from the struts.

I sensed someone near me before I heard the sound of soft-soled shoes on gravel. I turned. A small white man, with an easy to forget face and nondescript brown hair, who I would have never noticed but for the black, ugly, and menacing looking .45 caliber automatic in his right hand, stood there about ten feet away, smiling a nondescript smile at me. The .45 was pointed at a spot on the roof a few feet in front of me, but I knew that was a condition that could quickly change.

"Well," the soft voice said. "Looks like Mo and Skeeter let you whup their asses again. I saw what you did to Skeeter. That wasn't nice, throwin' him off the roof like that."

22.

As situations go, I'd probably never been in a worse one.

The gunman was too far away for me to rush him. I had tranquilizer darts and a dart gun, but the darts weren't in the gun, making them less than useless. I couldn't pick Mo up and throw him at the guy; he was closer to Mo's body than I was. There *was* the shotgun lying there in the gravel, about three feet away. He could empty the .45 into me before I could pick it up.

Not a very promising situation. And, .45 caliber slugs do a lot of damage to the body. I'd just turned fifty, and for all my complaining, I was looking forward to fifty-one and beyond.

"The girls are gone," I said. "If you know what's good for you, you'll let me go as well."

"There's a problem with that, you see," he said. "You done caused the boss a whole lot of trouble, and he kinda wants you dead."

"You don't really think you can kill me and get away with it, do you? There are witnesses up there on that hotel roof."

"Oh, they ain't goin' nowhere, and they ain't witnessin' nothin'. Soon's we get rid of them suckers in front of the buildin', some of the boys will go over and retrieve them. The two broads'll be a little fun before we off 'em. The girls go back into the stable. See, no witnesses. You'll just disappear."

The sounds from the street in front of the building grew louder. In the distance, though, I could hear the wail of sirens, and they were coming closer.

"Sounds to me like you might have some unexpected company soon," I said.

He cocked his head. The sirens were nearer now. A frown creased his face.

"That ain't gonna help you. I'll just tell the cops I caught you trespassing." He looked down at the shotgun. "In fact, you tried to shoot me with that shotgun. I had to shoot in self-defense."

That didn't sound good – not good at all. Well, I thought, the only good defense is a strong, unexpected offense. The last thing he had to be expecting was for me to come at him, what with him having a clip full of ammo no doubt, and me having nothing but my bare hands.

Of course, he neglected to watch my feet. Who looks at a guy's feet when you're about to shoot him? Nobody, that's who. And, that was his undoing.

I dug my right toe into the gravel and kicked up and out, sending a cloud of rocky pebbles directly into his face. Some of them must have hit the surface of his eyes, because he yelled and threw his left hand up over his eyes and stepped backward. The gun wavered in his hand, but was pointing to the side instead of at me.

"Aw, you son of a bitch, you hit me in the eye," he said, rubbing at his eyes.

I stepped forward, three long strides, and brought my left leg up, to the right and then in a sweeping motion to the left, catching his wrist and sending the gun flying across the roof. I continued the move left; planting my left foot and bringing my right leg up, pulled back and then shot out in a stiff kick to his upper chest, sending him reeling backwards. He ended up sitting on his backside.

He rubbed at his eyes with both hands, and then looked up at me. I was already moving toward him. He scrambled backwards, and then scurried to his right, trying to work around toward his gun. I'm fast, but he was faster. He did a tuck and roll, and came up with the gun in his fist. I came to a sudden halt and dropped to a crouch.

As he swung around to aim at me, I reached down and took the knife from the ankle sheath, and with a quick overhand movement, threw it. It hit him in the throat, burying itself a good four inches. Blood welled around the blade. He dropped the .45 and grabbed at his throat, sinking backward and to his knees.

He looked at me, a pleading, disbelieving look in his eyes as he slowly toppled sideways, and then rolled over on his back. Blood was beginning to seep from between his lips.

I walked over and kicked the gun away. I then knelt beside him.

"I don't know anyone who's ever survived a wound like this, friend," I said. "You want to tell me your name so I can tell the undertaker."

Okay, that's pretty cold. The guy was fading fast, and here I was cracking wise. In fairness, though, if our roles had been reversed, he might have done the same. Even dying, though, he didn't give an inch.

He looked up at me; hatred in his now beginning to glaze over eyes; and tried to spit at me. It only resulted in a glob of bright red blood spilling out and over his cheek.

His lips moved spasmodically, but finally he gathered enough strength, and said, "Fuck you." And then, the life left his eyes.

I pulled my knife from his throat, and wiped it clean on his trouser leg, and left him there, and went back to the rope and tackle. I finished untying the rope and got up on the edge of the roof. Grasping the rope tightly, I stepped off the roof. I sailed across the eight foot gap, and hit the wall of the hotel hard. Fortunately, I kept my feet together and bent my knees to absorb some of the shock. It hurt like hell nonetheless.

Blood reached over and hauled on the rope to help me up the wall, and then grabbed my shoulders to pull me onto the hotel roof. I lay there breathing hard.

"That was pretty impressive," he said. "Pretty damned impressive if I do say so myself."

"Yeah, I guess it was," I said when I could catch my breath. "Where are the girls?"

"Over by the door. Figured it best they not see what was happening over on that other roof, just in case you couldn't handle that guy."

"Thanks for the vote of confidence."

"Oh, I have every confidence in you, son," he said. "I don't think you'd want them to see what you finally did to him either, would you?"

"No, I guess not. Let's get the gear stowed and get the hell out of here. The police have arrived, and I don't want to have to explain why we're here."

"Yes, the police are indeed here," he said. "And, while you were fighting off that assassin and playing the daring young man on the flying trapeze, they brought things under control."

Now that the ringing in my ears had subsided I did notice it was much quieter than before.

"Good," I said. "Now, let's get the hell out of here."

23.

As we passed through the lobby, Blood removed the desk clerk from the janitor's closet and placed him back on the stool behind the desk. I wondered what the poor man would think when he finally woke up.

We must have looked a sight as we exited the hotel; me in front carrying the bag, Heather, Lila, and the three girls behind me, and Blood bringing up the rear. I looked like I'd been in a fight – several fights – with scraped arms, my pants were torn at the knee, and I was covered with dust.

But, the chaos on the sidewalk was such that no one noticed us at first. Then, Elwood Tucker spotted Lila and her daughter, and came bounding over.

"Kitty, baby," he shouted. "You okay. They

didn't hurt you, did they?"

He gathered the two in an embrace. I noticed that the girl clung tightly to him, as did her mother. He released them and turned to me.

"Mr. Pennyback, I owe you big time. Thank you for savin' my family."

"Family?" Lila said. "Do that mean what I think it mean?"

"You gone finally be my daddy for real?" Jeanne asked.

"Damn straight I am," he said. "That is, if yo momma will have me. Lila, honey, will you marry me?"

She said nothing; just grabbed the little man and stuck a yard of tongue down his throat. A few of the homeys near us cheered.

"All's well that ends well," Blood said.

"I think it's sweet," said Heather.

"Now," I said, looking down at the two girls we'd rescued. "We have to figure out what to do with these two. I guess we'll have to turn them over to the cops to find their parents."

They looked at me in wide-eyed fear.

"Don't you worry," Heather said. "Children Protective Services will take good care of you until they find your folks. I have a friend who works there, and I'll make sure of it."

Heather has a friend in every agency in the Washington area, and she probably could make sure of it. It seemed to ease their minds.

A commotion from in front of O'Grady's place drew my attention.

I looked over and saw Buster Mayweather standing in front of Seamus O'Grady's corpulent form. Buster looked angry, while O'Grady had put on his best snake oil salesmen's face.

"I assure you officer, my men did not start this altercation," he said. "This bunch of rowdys was creating a disturbance outside my place of business, and I merely asked my employees to ask them to disperse."

"Why didn't you just call the police?" Buster asked. "Your guys were waving guns around."

He pointed at a group of five men in handcuffs being led to a waiting police van.

"I'm willing to bet when we check, they won't have carry permits, and you know DC gun laws don't allow private citizens to have guns in public. This ain't Virginia, you know."

"Yes, officer," O'Grady said patiently. "I understand that, and I'm terribly distressed. They will, of course, have to take their punishment for breaking the law. I will get them the best legal representation, but I understand that you have to do your duty."

As I walked over, I could see the smug, self-satisfied look on his fat face, and all I wanted to do was smash it. When he saw me, the look vanished for an instant, but then returned.

"Hey, Al," Buster said. "What you doin' in this part of town? No, don't answer; I probably don't want to know."

"I just happened to be in the neighborhood when I heard all the commotion," I said. "I think, though, that you'll be glad I was here."

"Why is that, bro?"

"Because, I have what you'll need to arrest Mr. O'Grady here."

O'Grady's pig-like eyes went wide, and his cheeks reddened. Buster looked interested.

"Oh, yeah; and just what might that be?" Buster asked.

I turned and pointed at Heather and the others who were still standing in front of the hotel.

"For starters," I said. "There's a charge of kidnapping. Heather there was one of the victims, and I do believe she'll be happy to testify. So will the others, including three girls under the age of eighteen. Which brings up the really good charge – child prostitution. This tub of lard was holding those three kids in rooms upstairs against their will, and selling their services to people."

O'Grady had turned pale now. Buster was smiling broadly.

"Well now, don't that just beat all? Seamus O'Grady, I'm arresting you for kidnapping, assault, conspiracy to commit assault, and soliciting prostitution of minors, or whatever the hell that charge is. You have the right to remain silent, and I recommend you keep your fat mouth shut; you have the right to the services of an attorney, and if you cannot afford an attorney, one will be appointed for you. Do you understand these rights that I've explained to you?"

The fat man just glared at him.

"I take that as a yes," Buster said. "Now, turn yo fat ass around while I slap some plasti-cuffs on you."

Buster, not too gently, spun O'Grady around and secured his pudgy wrists with the plastic handcuffs, giving them an extra tug, which caused the fat man to wince.

"I hope that hurt, fucker," Buster said quietly over O'Grady's shoulder. "I been waitin' a long time for this." He beckoned one of the uniformed officers standing near. "Put this one in the back of the squad car over there."

"Sure thing, detective," the officer said, and taking his cue from Buster's handling of the man, manhandled him toward the waiting car.

"I guess there'll be some celebrating in the police department today," I said.

"Bet yo ass there will. We been after that fuck for a long time. So, he snatched Heather, did he? That was pretty stupid of him, messin' with somebody close to you like that."

"Worse, the son of a bitch called me and told me," I said.

Buster looked over my shoulder at Blood, who had remained unobtrusively in the shade of the hotel canopy.

"So, you and Blood there come huntin' for bear?"

"Something like that."

"What kind of damage you do inside?"

"Well, there are two . . . no, three unconscious men in the alley; an unconscious man and a stiff on the roof." I pointed up. "You'll also find a shotgun and a couple of handguns on the roof."

Buster shook his head. "Damn, bro; for a guy who don't carry a piece, you sho leave a lot of bodies layin' 'round. I know it was self-defense, but gone have to get a statement from you later anyway."

I agreed.

"The two girls with Heather will need foster care until their parents can be found."

"Don't sweat it," he said. "They're on the way."

"Okay, we'll wait around for that, and then, if you don't need me for anything, I need to get Heather home."

Buster pointed to a tough looking female cop who was standing in front of a crowd of curious onlookers.

"No need of that," he said. "Hey, Officer Winston, I need you over here." The woman jogged over and saluted him. "I need you to take custody of those two minors over there and take care of them until Child Services arrives."

"Sure thing, detective," she said, and saluted again before walking over to Heather.

As she approached the children, her demeanor changed. She was no longer the tough looking cop, but a gentle looking lady who just happened to be wearing riot gear. She took the two girls by the hand and led them toward an empty cop car.

"Okay, bro," Buster said. "You can get the

hell out of here now."

"Sure thing, detective," I said.

I saluted and left.

24.

Things got busy after that.

First, we had to go to the precinct and give our statements. Blood and I didn't go into too much detail about our activities, especially the part about drugging the hotel desk clerk, and I was told that I wasn't likely to be prosecuted for killing the guy on the roof, given the circumstances. Heather and Lila gave their accounts of being snatched from Heather's house, and the three girls, with a Juvenile Services Officer present, described what they'd been told about plans for them.

After reading and signing our statements, we were allowed to leave. Blood went with me to take Heather home. I told her to take a few days off, which she surprised me by agreeing to do.

Then, we went back to his place. I retrieved Sandra and went home, leaving Blood to explain the morning's activity to Elizabeth. I had enough to do explaining to Sandra, and felt it would be easier to do on home ground. She was so happy that I'd come out of it all with only a few scratches, she didn't fuss at me as she usually does. We didn't come up for air until the following day.

On Saturday, the phone started ringing. First, Tucker called to say that he'd learned that he had to wait until Monday to file for a marriage license, and it wouldn't be issued until Thursday, but he and Lila planned to go to a Justice of the Peace and get married as soon as they'd picked it up. He wanted me to be his best man, and Lila was insisting that Heather be her maid of honor.

I agreed, and decided to extend my time off to cover the whole of the following week. It's not as if we had any pressing business. When I called Heather, she sounded groggy, but agreed to take the week off, and perked up when I told her about being maid of honor at a wedding.

I'd no sooner got off the phone with her when Buster called.

"Hey, bro," he said. "Sorry to bother you, but I thought you'd like to hear the news."

"What news?" I asked.

"If you'd watch TV or subscribe to a newspaper, you'd know," he said.

"I listen to radio; I just haven't had time today."

"Yeah, I know what you been doin'. No matter; the news is that O'Grady's finally goin' down, and I mean down in a big way. DA's goin' for five counts of kidnappin', which is good for thirty years on each count, and then abducting minors for the purpose of commercial sex, which is good for twenty years on each, and then the general prostitution charge, while it don't carry a lot of jail time, lets the city seize all property used in the business. That means the club *and* the hotel. Some of his goons, seein' the way the wind's blowin', been singin' like canaries. Man, we got this sucker, and we got him good."

"That's good news," I said. "He'll finally pay for all the years he's been abusing people."

"It gets even better. Because of the recent interest in child prostitution, the feds want a piece of him too. This dude will be behind bars when my kids are gray-haired; that is, if he lives that long. You know how cons hate child abusers. He's apt to get a shiv stuck in his fat gut the first time he takes a shower."

"Excuse me if I don't seem too sympathetic to his plight. He'll deserve whatever he gets."

"Amen to that, bro. I'll let you get back to whatever it was you were doin'. Just wanted to share the good news. I figured you'd be interested."

I thanked him and rang off. Sandra had been lying quietly on the bed as I talked. When I put the phone back on the bedside table, she reached over and pulled me down next to her.

"Want to tell me what that call was about?" she murmured into my ear.

"Do you want me to tell you now, or would you rather wait until afterwards?"

"Afterwards? After what?"

I snaked my hand down along her thigh. She murmured some more.

"Oh, after that?"

"Yeah, that. Still want to know what the call was about?"

"What call?"

The good news got better.

EPILOGUE

The week went by all too fast.

On Thursday, Sandra and I picked Heather up at home and drove downtown to the office of a Justice of the Peace who had agreed to perform the wedding ceremony for Elwood James Tucker and Lila Marie Logan.

Tucker had cleaned himself up passably well. He'd gotten his hair cut conservatively short and from somewhere had procured a dark blue suit that made him look like a relatively up and coming business man – almost; there was still a bit of the street in the way he dipped when he walked. Lila, on the other hand, looked radiant. She wore a powder blue pants suit, with a large white rose pinned to the lapel. She'd had her hair done and wore just a hint of makeup, which set off her golden complexion. Jeanne was the spitting image of her mother; same hair style, and same light blue suit. The kid would be a knockout when she filled out. Tucker, even before the vows were exchanged, was acting the part of her father, giving the evil eye to any male under forty who looked too long at her.

Buster dropped in before the ceremony to let Tucker know that no one had mentioned his name in connection with any of O'Grady's illegal activities, and as long as he stayed straight, he was okay. Lila assured Buster that her 'man' would be getting a regular job. No more collecting vig or running numbers for him. He agreed, saying that a man had to set a good example for his child.

I actually felt proud of the little rodent, going so far as to call him Mouse rather than Elwood, or Mr. Tucker. We'd never be drinking buddies, but I had to admire his determination to pull himself and his new family out of the gutter that he'd been in for so long.

After the ceremony was over, with Tucker almost forgetting to say, 'I do,' and having to be prompted twice by the JP, we said our goodbyes. We dropped Heather back at her place and headed home.

We were just crossing Key Bridge when Sandra laid a hand softly on my arm.

"Al, before we go home, could we go up to Woodley Park?" she said.

"Sure, babe; but, why do you want to go up there? Traffic's pretty bad this time of day going up Connecticut Avenue."

"I know, but it's really important. I'll tell you when we get there. It's not too far from the zoo, and we can get home from there without much problem."

When she bats those baby blues at me like she was doing, I find it hard to say no to her. They say Helen of Troy's face launched a thousand ships; I'll lay you dollars to doughnuts, she had blue eyes, and it was actually the batting of her lush lashes that put all those warships into the water.

"Okay, but you know I really *don't* like surprises."

She squeezed my arm, a gentle squeeze.

"That's because you've never gotten a proper surprise."

"I'm not sure there is such a thing."

"Trust me, babe, there is; there truly is. Now, just drive."

Easier said than done. I had to make a quick decision about routing. From Georgetown to Woodley Park, it's hell any way you go, but I decided to try my luck with M Street. Fortunately, I was in the bridge's center lane, and only had to cut off a mini-van to get over into the right lane for the right turn on M Street. I got caught by the light, and had to wait, enduring the waving and middle-digit pointing of the buy in the van. At least he didn't blow his horn, which would have really pissed me off.

After the light turned green, I turned onto M Street, and crawled along in bumper-to-bumper traffic until I crossed Rock Creek. After that, the street widened and the traffic thinned out, so it was a smooth drive to Thirty-Third Street, just west of the sprawling and ever-expanding George Washington University campus, where I turned left. I drove north, went around Washington Circle and then northeast on New Hampshire to Dupont Circle, and then north on Connecticut.

Sandra was consulting directions on a little piece of paper, and when we got to California Avenue, just south of the National Zoo, she instructed me to turn left. After a few blocks, we came to Massachusetts Avenue, where she told me to turn right. Her cheeks turned red when she realized that we could have gotten on Massachusetts instead of Connecticut at Dupont Circle, and saved ourselves a few stop signs. I just smiled and shrugged.

We crossed Rock Creek again, and she had me turn on to Whitehaven Street. Finally, she spotted a narrow paved drive on the right and directed me to turn there.

I entered a winding, one-lane pathway with trees and shrubs crowding it on both sides, that snaked its way uphill for what seemed like half a mile before coming to the top of the hill, in front of a two-story, red-brick colonial with arched windows and a porte cochere in front. The drive wound beneath the overhang at the front, and around the left side of the house.

I pulled up under the porte cochere, and we got out. Sandra pressed the little gold button beside the dark wooden double front doors. I heard chimes somewhere in the distance playing Beethoven's *fur Elise.*

The doors swung inward, and there stood a slight built man with iron gray hair combed severely back on his square head, steel blue eyes under neatly trimmed gray brows, and the pink complexion of someone who doesn't spend a lot of time in the sun. He was dressed in sharply creased gray trousers, a dark blue blazer with gold buttons, and a powder blue silk shirt, open at the throat, showing a clump of curly gray hair. I put him in his eighties at least.

"Yes," he said in a quiet, cultured voice. "May I help you?"

"I'm Sandra Winter," Sandra said. "And, you must be Alistair Wingate? We spoke on the phone yesterday."

"Ah, yes, Ms. Winter." He proffered an

immaculately manicured hand. "I've been expecting you. Won't you come in?"

"Thank you, Mr. Wingate. We won't take up too much of your time."

"Nonsense; I'm glad for the company. And, please, do call me Alistair, or just Al. No need for such formality."

He stepped back to let us enter, looking me over as I passed him.

"Very well, Alistair," she said. "This is Al Pennyback. I told you about him on the phone."

"Of course; I should have known." He offered me his hand. He had a firm, dry grip, but his skin felt thin like parchment. "Pleased to meet you, Mr. Pennyback."

"You can just call me Al," I said.

"Al; is that short for Alfred or Albert?"

"Albert; but I much prefer Al."

"I know the feeling," he said. "I've always felt that Alistair is much too pretentious. But, I guess it would be confusing for Ms. Winter to have to deal with two Al's, now wouldn't it?"

Sandra laughed. "You can say that again. And, please just call me Sandra."

Al, Al, and Sandra; like an old rock singing group. Everyone smiled.

"Very well, Sandra," he said. "I suppose you'll be wanting to see the merchandise?"

"If it's no bother. We don't want to take up too much of your time."

"I was hoping you might have a cup of tea with me."

He looked like someone who had more money than all the banks in the area could count, but the look in his eyes was that of a man who had no friends or family, and who longed for someone to just 'sit and have a cup of tea.'

"I see no problem with that," I said.

His face lit up like a kid who just learned that there *is* a Santa Claus.

"Oh, good; I've already set the tea service out. It's right this way."

He led us through an entrance foyer that a moving van could have parked in and not touched the walls, into an even larger room filled with expensive wooden furniture and vases that looked as if they should be on display in the Smithsonian. For a man of his wealth, it struck me as strange that he had no servants. Sandra must have also been curious.

"You don't have any household help?" she asked.

"Oh, no," he said. "Not since my wife died last year. It was just too much of a reminder of her having them around, and they were always fussing over me. I have a lady who comes in twice a week to clean, but I do everything else myself."

I looked around. The place was huge, and had more places to dust than I could count. Someone coming in twice a week wouldn't even be able to keep up with the dust. He seemed a nice enough old chap, but odd – definitely odd. I couldn't put my finger on it, though.

A glass and marble coffee table sat in front of a couch that was covered in a velvety brown fabric. An ornate silver tea service, with fragile china cups and saucers sat atop the table. He poured the steaming brown liquid into three cups.

"Would you like anything with it?" he asked as he handed Sandra a cup. "I have sugar, milk and lemon. You know, I lived a few years in London, and developed a taste for sugar and milk in my tea. Most Americans think it's an odd way to drink it, but that's just because they've never tried it like that."

He handed me a cup.

"Thanks, but I like mine black," I said.

"Just a half spoon of sugar," Sandra said.

He put two spoons of sugar in his; and

enough milk to almost turn it white. As I watched him stir the milk in I realized where the British expression 'white coffee' comes from. I took a sip of my tea. I didn't recognize it. All I knew was that it didn't come from the local super market, or from one of those little tissue bags that you dip in hot water.

"Nice flavor," I said.

"It's Darjeeling. I have it shipped from India."

"Nice," Sandra said.

He sipped his daintily, looking over the rim of his cup at Sandra and me. He didn't say anything; just sipped his tea with a contented look on his face. All he wanted was company, not conversation. Strange old guy, I thought.

Finally, he put his cup down. "Sorry I didn't offer you biscuits with your tea," he said. "I'm afraid that's one English custom I didn't adopt. At my age, I don't need the extra carbohydrates, you know."

I looked at him strangely, but then remembered; biscuits are what the English call cookies. They call biscuits scones. A different name for everything. It's true what they say; America and England are two societies separated by a common language. He seemed to move from one to the other with ease, though. Wow, a polyglot in English.

"That's perfectly fine," Sandra said. "You

really didn't have to do this. We should conclude our business and get out of your hair."

The old guy was nice, but I sensed that Sandra wasn't completely comfortable with him. Being around kids all day during the school year and around me most of the rest of the time, she hadn't had all that much contact with the really old. When I worked the case of the elderly lady who'd been murdered in a senior citizens' home, she hadn't had much contact with them. Now that I was approaching senior citizen status, I wondered if she'd become uncomfortable with me. I'd have to remember to ask her one day.

If Wingate detected her discomfort, he didn't let it show. He continued to smile at us.

"Yes, you're right," he said. "I forget sometimes that you young people can never sit in one place too long. Shall we have a look at the goods?"

Sandra put her cup on the table and stood. I stood as well, but finished the rest of my tea before putting the cup down. The old guy struck me as strange, but likeable, and the tea was good.

He walked us through the living room – or, maybe he called it a parlor – through an even larger dining room with a table in the center you could play basketball on under a chandelier with more glass and crystal than Macy's, and out through a large plate glass door onto a patio that had been done in pastel colored stone slabs. Directly behind the house, across a manicured expanse of lawn – I reckon he had a lawn service, because I couldn't see him mowing that much grass – was a large, one-story building that must have been a hundred yards wide, with twenty doors.

"Is that what I think it is?" I asked.

"I'm not sure what you think it is," he said. "But, it's a garage."

It was one hell of a garage.

"Is there a car behind every door?"

"No; some of the vehicles are small, so there are two in four of the stalls."

I did some quick math; that meant twenty-four cars. Even for a rich guy, that was a lot of wheels. My mouth popped open.

"Oh, I don't drive them all," he said with a smile. "I'm a collector. I just like having them around."

The grass underfoot as we walked across the lawn was as soft as an expensive carpet. We stepped onto the driveway which came around the house and ran the width of the garage, serving as both a driveway and a parking apron.

Wingate walked to the left door and opened it with a large brass key that he'd taken from his jacket pocket. He pulled on the handle and the door slid easily up and tucked into the ceiling. He reached inside and flipped a light switch and invited us to enter.

It was like walking into a car museum, or the Ford Museum in Dearborn, Michigan, which I visited once when I was working with a reserve army unit in Detroit. Shiny vintage and antique cars stretched the entire width of the building. There were no 'stalls' as such, but white lines painted on the concrete floor marked the parking spaces.

The first car was a beaut, and really brought back my visit to Dearborn. It was a 1930 Ford Model A Tudor, painted in a dark blue finish, with green and black upholstered fabric seats. The tires looked shiny and new. Next to it was a 1953 lemon yellow Lincoln Capri with a black top and white sidewall tires. As we moved down the line, I could hear Sandra's gasping intake of breath as we neared each vehicle. I could understand how she was feeling. I was impressed myself.

The third car was a 1934 Bentley DHC. The finish was a deep red, with an almost purple top, and acres of shiny chrome. As I passed the front of the Bentley, I stopped in my tracks. My breath caught in my throat.

I couldn't believe what I was seeing. It sat there, like a hunchback, hidden from view by the other, larger cars; crouching between the Bentley and a 1961 blue Austin Healey 3000 Mk2. It was lime green, and the exterior was blemish-free. Its nose poked out, and the flattened back emphasized the humped top.

Now, I think I knew what Sandra's secret surprise was. I felt the sting of salt in my eyes. She walked up behind me and put her arms around my waist.

"Well, babe," she said. "What do you think of it?

It was a 1963 Volkswagen Beetle; looking as if it had just rolled off the assembly line. It had black wall tires, instead of the white walls that had been popular when it was first built, and the tires looked as if they'd never been driven. It wasn't my old Brown Bomber, but damn it, it was a close cousin. *It* was beautiful.

"It's beautiful," I said.

Wingate came up beside me.

"When Ms. Win -, er, Sandra, contacted me and said you might want a Volkswagen, I was more than happy to deal with her. I've been needing to make room for another acquisition I'm contemplating, and if I can make someone else happy in doing so, well, so much the better."

I turned around and cupped Sandra's face in my hands.

"Sandra, babe, this must have cost a fortune. I can't let you spend your money like that."

"It didn't cost much, Al, honey," she said. "Just twelve thousand."

My mouth dropped open again. I'm no expert on antique cars, but that seemed low for a vintage Beetle in such good condition. I turned to Wingate with a question in my eyes.

"That's right, Al," he said, raising his hands. "I'm selling it to her for what I paid for it. It's not like I need the money."

"I don't know what to say," I said.

"How about a simple, thank you," Sandra said.

"Thank you," I said.

"I'm just sorry I didn't have it in brown," Wingate said. "Sandra said your original Volkswagen was brown."

"That's no problem. The color isn't important; it's the car that matters." I turned to Sandra. "How did you find it?"

"I just happened to be reading a local shopper's paper," she said. "And, I saw Mr. Wingate's . . . Alistair's . . . ad offering a

Volkswagen Beetle for sale. I called him a couple of days before your birthday and made an offer."

"She got me on my mobile phone," he said. "Unfortunately, I was in Chicago taking care of some family business, and only returned to Washington a few days ago."

"So, this is the surprise you had for me?"

"Yes. I know how much you loved that old car. I saw the look in your eyes when it was blown up. I've been putting a little away every payday since. Your fiftieth birthday seemed a good occasion to present it to you. Are you happy?"

I pulled her close, smelling the aroma of lilac shampoo in her hair, and feeling the warmth of her body against mine.

"I love it, babe. This is the best birthday present anyone's ever given me. In fact, next to you, it's the best thing that's ever happened to me."

Wingate made a slight coughing noise.

"As much as I hate to break up such a beautiful scene, perhaps we should go back inside and complete the transaction."

I pulled away from her – reluctantly – and followed him back to the house. I could still feel her warmth. Back in the dining room, we completed the transfer of ownership, and Sandra gave him a check. He handed me the pink slip and a set of keys.

"Well, she's now yours," he said. "May you have many happy miles of driving her. You know, I've never driven it myself. In fact, I've only driven one or two of them."

"You missed a treat," I said. "Pound for pound, the Beetle is one of the best cars on the road. Hitler and his goons might have been evil, but they knew how to make a damn fine car. Is it gassed up and ready to go?"

"It has a full tank, and I had it completely checked out and lubricated. You can drive it home if you like."

Oh, yes – I like, I thought.

"Will you be giving it a name?" Sandra asked.

I thought about it for a moment or two. It could never replace the Brown Bomber, so giving it a similar name wouldn't do. It represented a new phase, so a new name was in order. My new Beetle, my little lime green bug car. And, just like that, the name popped into my head.

"It'll be the Bug," I said.

"Not exactly an impressive name," Wingate said. "But, appropriate."

He escorted us to the door. I gave Sandra the keys to the Mustang.

"You want me to follow or lead?" I asked.

"You lead, of course," she said.

"I'll leave you two now," Wingate said. We shook hands. "Take care and be happy. Just close the garage door when you leave. I'll lock it later."

He went back inside and closed the door.

Sandra and stood there, our shoulders touching. At that moment, I think I loved her more than I could express in words. She, like the new Volkswagen, was a part of my new life. I pulled her into my arms, and our lips met.

We kissed deeply, drinking of each other's essence, our bodies melting into a single entity. It was a long and loving kiss; a kiss of warmth; a kiss of love. It was a kiss of life.

About the Author

Charles Ray has been writing fiction since his teens, winning a national Sunday school magazine writing contest while still in junior high school. He has worked as a newspaper and magazine journalist during the 60s and 70s, contributing articles, reviews, photographs, and artwork to publications in the US and abroad. His first full length work was a book on leadership, *Things I Learned from My Grandmother About Leadership and Life*, published in 2008. In 2009, he began writing fiction again, with the first in the Al Pennyback mystery series, *Color Me Dead*. He has since published more than 30 works of fiction and non-fiction.

A native of Texas who now calls Maryland home, he served 20 years in the army, and upon retirement joined the US Foreign Service, serving as a diplomat in more than six countries, and dealing with scores of others. Since his retirement from public service in 2012, he has devoted most of his time to writing and public speaking.

For more information on his published works, check his author page at: http://www.amazon.com/Charles-Ray/e/B006WMLEZK or follow his tweets at http://www.twitter.com/charlieray45.

www.ingramcontent.com/pod-product-compliance
Lightning Source LLC
Chambersburg PA
CBHW070837120626
46556CB00002B/782